Laura

STORM BODIES

Steve Orme

Hope this book goes down
a storm!
Best wishes

To Marcus,

an inspiration who made this possible

1

IT WAS the smell that Dan Forsyth had never got used to –
but this was like nothing he'd ever sniffed before.

He wasn't bothered by the muck, the dust and the
thought of what people might have put in their dustbins. It
was a dirty job, yes – but someone had to do it.

He'd been doing it for eighteen years now, lugging
bins up and down the street, making sure they were emptied
properly, returning them to their rightful owners and putting
up with barbed comments from self-centred people who
weren't satisfied with the service the council provided.

Straight after a shift he'd have a shower, wash his hair
and change his clothes. Initially he'd done it merely to pacify
his wife; now he did it because he needed to feel refreshed.
He enjoyed seeing the grime that had engulfed him during
the day as it washed down the plughole.

But as soon as he was back at the depot the following
morning, the smell returned as strong as ever.

He'd tried everything to get rid of it: he'd started the
day wearing a surgical mask only to discard it after a few
minutes because his glasses steamed up; he'd risked being the
butt of his colleagues' jokes by turning up one morning
reeking of a costly aftershave; and on one occasion he'd gone

to work with a raging hangover after several pints and whisky chasers during a prolonged pub crawl. But still the smell wouldn't go away.

He'd contemplated making an appointment with his GP. But all his doctor would probably say was 'you've got sensitive nostrils. Live with it.'

It wasn't as if he had the enhanced smell of a superhero. He couldn't detect whether anyone was lying or if someone had a tumour simply because of the aroma they gave off.

He just happened to be the first to notice when an unusual or a particularly pungent smell was in the air.

He didn't expect anything out of the ordinary when the refuse lorry pulled into a nondescript street of terraced and semi-detached houses in the Aspley district of Nottingham. The bins were all in their proper place, lined up on the edge of the pavement, waiting to disgorge their contents into the truck.

He was rushing around more quickly than usual as big spots of rain began to fall, forcing him to zip up his council-issue waterproof even though it didn't keep him completely dry.

He almost didn't notice a black, battered, extra large suitcase. Dan knew it was the council's policy not to take anything that didn't fit inside a bin – but he preferred to use common sense rather than stick to the rules.

The suitcase was outside number 11, the home of Violet Campbell, a frail, harmless spinster who was well into her eighties. He thought it might have been a long time since she went travelling; and why would she need such a large case?

'Hey, Dan, shall we chuck it in the lorry?' one of his colleagues shouted.

'Yeah, can't do any harm. She's a sweet old lady. Probably hasn't got anyone to take it to the tip for her.'

But the closer Dan got to the case the more anxious he became as his nostrils picked up a smell: a cross between rotting fruit and raw sewage with a hint of a budget-priced perfume. He began to retch, the sickening odour lingering in his mouth and throat as well as sticking to his nasal hair.

He covered his nose with his sleeve but it made little difference. The stench grew even more sour and acerbic, forcing Dan to reconsider whether he should bother with the case. But if Violet wanted it taking away, how could he not be a good Samaritan?

He grabbed the handle and lifted. It took him most of his not inconsiderable strength to get the case off the floor.

'Bloody hell! Has she got a body in here?'

2

Miles Davies drove into the car park at the Cloud Centre, the name chosen for Derby Storm's impressive home venue because it was sponsored by a major IT company. It was the envy of most of the clubs in the British Basketball League.

There were few cars around during the early part of the day, so the detective inspector had plenty of freshly painted spaces to choose from as his eight-year-old motor glided over the newly laid tarmac.

He pulled up the collar of his coat as he walked the short distance to the main building, the north wind battering his face and reminding him that winter was close.

Miles sauntered up to the ticket desk which led to the basketball arena on one side and the club's Fast Break coffee shop on the other.

A smell of fresh paint took him by surprise. The centre was only a couple of years old but the owner was fastidious about making the right impression. He'd had the reception area spruced up for the new season in the team's signature colour, teal.

'Hello, Miles! Don't usually see you here during the day.'

Daisy Higgins sat upright behind the gleaming counter. With her blond hair cut delicately in a bob, crisp white blouse and elegant business suit, she looked the perfect ambassador as she welcomed everyone into the arena.

Daisy was more than just a member of the team who took a turn on reception. The owner could always rely on her to offer an astute opinion on his decisions rather than blindly following his orders. And although she was only just over five feet tall, she wasn't overawed by any of the club's huge players.

'That's normally because I don't get the chance to come over here unless there's a game on.'

Daisy checked as an ominous thought popped into her head.

'You're not here on official business, are you?'

'No, I'm on a day off. I need a couple of extra tickets for tonight. Can I swap my usual seats and get a block of five together? Some friends of mine are in town and I've persuaded them to come to a game. Should be a big crowd tonight.'

'It always is when Kingston are in town. I never got to watch them back in the 'eighties when they were among the best in Europe. But the current team's pretty good.

Hopefully we'll run them close. Will you be bringing your girlfriend with you?'

'Girlfriend? Who do you mean?'

'Tilly, of course. I thought you were an item.'

'No, we just share a love of the sport. I think it's never a good idea to have a relationship with someone you work with.'

There was a twinkle in Daisy's eye which Miles couldn't help but notice.

'You always look good together. And I've seen the way she watches you. That's not the way anyone looks at their boss. You're a detective – I reckon it's about time you examined the evidence in front of you. She's smitten.'

Miles felt uneasy, as awkward as he'd been the first time a defence barrister had tried to rip apart his testimony in a Crown Court trial.

'Uh, can I buy those tickets?'

Daisy decided not to embarrass him further and handed them over.

'We've only got a handful left. Kingston are bringing a couple of coach loads with them, so it should be a good atmosphere.'

'It's half term too,' said Miles, 'so we should have a lot of kids coming. Jordan will be here, so the Storm had better play well!'

Miles' young son normally missed evening games because he had to be up the following morning for school. Holidays though were special: Miles got to spend precious time with Jordan who loved watching basketball live.

'Have a good day off. See you later.'

'It'll be a great day if we can beat Kingston.'

3

The driver of the refuse lorry switched off the engine, unbuckled his seat belt, opened the door and jumped down. He had the same morbid curiosity as his colleagues who crowded around the unremarkable-looking suitcase.

They were like holidaymakers delighted to see their luggage emerge from an empty airport carousel after other sunseekers had already wheeled their trollies through arrivals. The workers, though, didn't expect the case would contain summer clothes or swimwear.

A man walking a small dog loitered to try to find out what was going on. Two women, one wearing a leisure suit and trainers, the other a well-worn dressing gown over pyjamas and shabby slippers, stopped their gossiping in case they missed a tale they could pass on to the whole neighbourhood.

'Go on, Dan, open it.'

The wind was getting stronger, trying to blow away the autumn rain that was falling faster and dissuading more passers-by from stopping for a look. Despite that, Dan's hands felt clammy and sweat began to trickle down his neck.

Torn between wanting to discover what was inside the case and an aversion to the smell which caused him to retch every few seconds, Dan inched forwards.

He hoped the case contained bricks or mortar that someone couldn't be bothered to dispose of in the correct way. But why would Violet Campbell have builders' rubble in a case? It didn't look as though tradesmen of any description had been anywhere near the property in the past couple of years; and if they had, surely they'd take their debris away with them?

Dan told himself to face up to the reality of what was actually in the case. Would it be kittens? A whole litter of puppies? Some people wouldn't be able to cope if they had half a dozen extra mouths to feed. Pet lovers could quickly become pet haters when presented with the results of their animal's amorous adventures.

But he'd never seen either a cat or a dog at Violet's. And why was the case so heavy?

He knew he couldn't put off opening it any longer.

'Get back, everyone.' His words were directed at his colleagues as much as the busybodies who had no business trying to get close to the mysterious object on the pavement. Their phones were at the ready as they prepared to picture the scene for their social media accounts.

'You look like one of those contestants on *Deal or No Deal*,' said the driver and his colleagues laughed. 'Come on, get the box open.'

Dan tugged at the first clasp which clicked as it snapped open.

The second one resisted, forcing him to exert as much pressure with his thumb as he could muster before it thudded out of its fastening.

He lifted the lid which creaked open before Dan flung it back onto the pavement. He recoiled, bringing up the sleeve of his luminous jacket to protect his nose from the noxious, nauseous stink.

One of the younger members of the collection team gagged, pulled away and deposited the remnants of a full English breakfast into the gutter.

The sight disgusted everyone, yet no one could take their eyes away from the decomposing, colourless, repulsive torso.

4

'Wow, this atmosphere is just amazing.' Stuart Bainbridge looked at Miles with gratitude and surprise as he, his partner Amy, Miles, his son Jordan and Tilly Johnson waited for the Storm to tip off against Kingston.

'Why didn't you tell me basketball was this exciting?'

Bainbridge and Amy had spent time with Miles and his ex-wife Lorraine before they split up. They still visited Derby as often as possible and Miles tried to coincide days off with their excursions to the East Midlands.

'I've been going on at you for years to come to a game,' Miles replied. 'You don't know what you've been missing.'

Bainbridge had been a detective inspector when Miles first moved into CID. The older man noticed that Miles showed potential and treated him like a son, encouraging him whenever he made headway in an investigation. But Bainbridge wasn't averse to censuring the young pretender whenever he stepped out of line.

Miles was distraught when Bainbridge retired at the first available opportunity, moving down south to be close to his elderly, infirm parents.

He also set up his own business, using all his experience in the police to become a corporate investigator. The services he offered included looking into drug use in the workplace, determining whether employees were stealing goods or information, and checking whether suppliers fraudulently billed their clients.

Bainbridge eased himself into his seat and wished he'd not been such a glutton at a Turkish restaurant Miles had booked them into for a pre-game meal.

His face, reddening after a quick dash up a flight of stairs, become even more crimson as he realised a lack of exercise and entertaining corporate bosses meant he was seriously overweight.

'Good seats, Miles. We can see all the action from here. So, who's going to win?'

'The Storm, of course!' shouted Jordan as the noise around them grew louder by the minute as Derby's supporters were relishing the start of the game.

Bainbridge turned to Miles for a more balanced view.

'It'll be tough. Kingston may not be as good as the old team – but I've got a feeling they'll be too good for Derby.'

'Of course, you'll remember them from first time around.'

'Cheeky bugger! Oh, Jordan, you shouldn't have heard that. I'll have you know, Stuart, that I was hardly out of nappies then. Mind you, I wish I'd been around to see that team. Any fans a bit older than me, they still talk about players like Steve Bontrager and Dan Davis. I've spent a good few hours watching them on YouTube. The footage is old but you can still see what quality players they were.'

The Storm were within touching distance of Kingston throughout the game. In the last couple of minutes, spurred on by a boisterous, sell-out crowd, they pulled away to record an unexpected and season-defining 82-71 win.

Bainbridge invited Miles and Tilly to his hotel for a nightcap. 'Sorry, Stuart.' The disappointment and regret could be heard clearly in Miles' voice. 'I've got to get Jordan home, then I need to go to bed. Early start tomorrow.'

'I know what it's like. It was relentless when I was in the force. I bet it's worse now.'

Miles gave a feeble smile. He loved his job – but there were times when work seemed like a treadmill set at a speed he was struggling to maintain.

Bainbridge then startled Miles. 'Look, why don't you jack it all in? Come and work with me! I've been thinking about expanding the business. We could have an East Midlands branch and you could run it. You'd do a great job.

'Just think: no more early-morning starts, no more calls at all times of the night when a major crime comes in. And, best of all: you could spend more time with Jordan. Don't give me your answer now – sleep on it.'

Detective Sergeant James West of the East Midlands Police was perplexed. He'd been summoned to the detective superintendent's office which he thought meant bad news.

Had he forgotten to file a report on one of the succession of crimes he'd dealt with in the past couple of weeks? Had he not made a strong enough case on one of his investigations which led to the Crown Prosecution Service throwing it out because of a lack of evidence?

Detective Superintendent Tom Brooksby, with his smart but conservative suit, white shirt and unostentatious tie all bought from a department store, didn't appear on a higher plain than his subordinates. His strong facial features and toned body gave him an air of authority – but he never abused his position.

'Sit down, James.' Brooksby tried to put the junior officer at ease.

West sat down on a cheap-looking yet comfortable chair opposite his boss.

The detective superintendent impressed staff with his caring attitude and his attempt to connect with them.

'How are things?'

West's heart rate began to slow down. 'Fine, thanks, sir. I reckon we're doing a decent job with limited resources.'

'That's what I want to talk to you about. Something's just come in. Pretty grim it is too. A headless torso discovered in a suitcase.

'All the DIs are busy, apart from your immediate gaffer Miles who's got a couple of days off. I need someone to be my right-hand man on the investigation. Fancy it?'

West's jaw almost ended up in his lap.

'Me, sir?'

'Why not? You've been a sergeant for a few years now. You ought to be thinking about taking your inspector's exams soon.'

West's eye widened and a smile erupted across his face.

'Thank you for your confidence in me, sir. What do I have to do?'

'Make sure that everything's done by the book in the initial stages. Employ staff wherever you think they're needed. Uniform have got a team going house to house. If you can think of anything better they could be doing, don't be afraid to redeploy them. Pull everything together and keep me posted. That okay?'

'Yes, sir! I won't let you down.'

'Oh, and one other thing: when you get a case like this, the national media is all over it. I expect we'll be getting journalists coming up here from London and doing all they can to get an exclusive. I need someone who can put them in their place and make sure any details that come out are issued in the proper way by the press office. Can you manage that?'

5

Miles dropped Jordan off at his mum's house, made polite conversation with his ex-wife Lorraine for a few minutes, then excused himself and headed home.

He tried to sleep but he couldn't settle: not only was he was exhilarated by the Storm's victory but also Stuart Bainbridge's words kept going round and round in his head: *'I've been thinking of expanding the business. We could have an East Midlands branch. You could run it. You'd do a great job.'*

Normally he wouldn't think twice about rejecting such an offer. But it had come shortly after he'd been called into the Chief Constable's office and been warned about his conduct.

He remembered every minute detail about his meeting with the Chief – he tried to put it out of his mind but it would come back at any moment, turning him into a melancholic mess.

It had been a similar day to the one that was nearly over: a concrete-coloured sky threatened rain and made everywhere look gloomy. Despite that, Miles was upbeat as he was shown into the Chief's office.

'Sit down, Miles.' The Chief sounded stern as he stood behind his desk, a deliberate move to emphasise his superiority.

Miles took in the surroundings, a plush, stylish environment that reeked of taste and elegance. Wonder how much this cost, he thought. Money that could have been used to fight the increase in crime that was devastating communities across the East Midlands.

'I need to talk to you about a serious problem. Your behaviour during the raid on Ken Thompson's house.'

Thompson had been the head of a lawless gang that had ruled the region for several years. He'd ordered the murder of three journalists who'd printed or broadcast stories that had denigrated his mother.

A firearms team had descended on his house only for him to take his cleaner hostage. It was intervention from Miles that had enabled armed officers to shoot and kill Thompson.

'What on earth were you thinking about, throwing a basketball at Thompson? Totally irresponsible.'

'I disagree, sir," said Miles, trying to hide the disdain and disrespect that was building up inside him. 'There was no chance that – '

'Anything could have happened. You could have hit one of the armed officers with that ball. They could have been distracted and pulled the trigger. Innocent people could have been injured – or worse.'

'With respect, sir, I threw the ball nowhere near those officers. I'd used footage from our drone to check out where everyone was. If I hadn't hit Thompson, the ball would have bounced near him and disrupted his concentration. The result would have been the same.'

'Well, not everyone thought that way. The firearms commander couldn't believe what he was seeing. He'd got Plan B ready to implement. We could have taken Thompson alive if you hadn't interfered.'

Miles had left the Chief Constable's office with a mixture of irritation, resentment, disappointment and anger that he'd been lambasted for his actions.

The force had referred Thompson's death to the Independent Office for Police Conduct. It took statements from everyone at the scene and studied footage from the body cameras of the firearms team as well as the drone footage. The IOPC found that officers 'acted in accordance with the relevant policies and procedures'.

An inquest recorded a verdict that Thompson was lawfully killed. Miles had no reservations about what he'd done. And if he were faced with a similar incident, he knew he'd behave in exactly the same way.

Maybe the Chief was bothered about the publicity that the story generated. Miles didn't want to exaggerate his part in the operation, but the press office convinced him it would show the police in a good light.

So that was how Miles was the subject of a full-page article in the East Midlands Express, holding a ball aloft and preparing to hurl it, as he did when he propelled it in Thompson's direction. He'd regretted it from the moment he picked up the paper and saw the staged picture.

He lay on one side, then the other. But sleep just wouldn't come. Would he really miss policing if he decided his career should go in a different direction? He was dedicated to his job, there was no doubt about it. The adrenalin he experienced when piecing together a new, complicated case was unique – better even than when he was playing basketball.

He knew private security wouldn't have the same buzz. But being able to spend more time with Jordan and watching him growing up was an almost irresistible pull.

Miles thought about some of the bad moves he'd made in his private life: getting married to Lorraine in the first place, splitting up with her and then having to watch as her boyfriend assumed the role of Jordan's dad. Thankfully the boyfriend had since disappeared.

Miles realised he had some difficult decisions to make.

6

Miles spent a quiet day off, tidying his house and catching up with some of the mundane jobs he usually forgot about when he was involved in a major investigation.

In the evening he met a few friends at a pub in Derby city centre, had a couple of pints and walked the short way home to his former railway worker's cottage near the railway station.

He was determined to get as much sleep as possible and had almost fallen into unconsciousness when his phone rang. He sprang up and looked at the display. He expected it would be the station calling him about a new case. But he was surprised to see the name Christine Hastings flash up before his tired but suddenly alert eyes.

Christine was Daisy Higgins' mum. A widow, she often helped Daisy to look after her seven-year-old son Joey. He was friends with Miles' son Jordan, the two of them occasionally having a sleepover at each other's house.

'Hello, Christine. Everything okay?'

'Oh, Miles, I'm so worried. Daisy hasn't come home yet.'

'Has she been out?'

'Yes. She always calls me if she's been delayed for any reason. But I've not heard a word from her.'

'Where did she go?'

'She went to a meeting about prisoners escaping from Sudbury. I thought it was a bit strange that she needed to go, but she told me some of the Storm players gave coaching lessons in a school in the village and she was concerned that the children might come across someone from the prison. I'm worried sick. I've called her on her mobile but there's no answer.

'Daisy's got one of those apps on her phone. You know, allows you to find out where people are. She set it up on my phone so that I can check where she is. I've gone on the app and all it says for her is "no location found".'

Fear gripped Miles but he composed himself, not wanting to pass on his concerns to Christine.

'Did she drive to the meeting?'

'Yes. She only had her car serviced last week, so I doubt if it's broken down anywhere. And if it had, she would have let me know.'

'Well, don't panic. I've known people whose car packed up on the same day that it was in the garage. And she might be in an area where mobile phone reception's a bit dodgy.

'Here's what I'll do. I'll call the control room and ask the duty inspector to brief any officers in the area to look out for her. You'll need to ring the police too. Tell them where Daisy went, what she was wearing, what time you were expecting her home. Give it ten minutes so that I can put the call in first. And try not to worry – we'll get it sorted.'

'That's kind of you, Miles. I'm so sorry to bother you with this.'

'Don't apologise. It's no bother. I'll let you know if I hear anything.'

Davies ended the call. He looked out of his bedroom window as rain which had been falling steadily throughout the evening had a new burst of life. Streams of water were beginning to gather pace as they headed for the nearest drain.

He knew sleep was out of the question. His years of experience in the police warned him that Daisy's non-arrival wouldn't have a positive ending.

7

No matter how many years Bill Cooper had left in the media industry, he knew he'd never get used to a modern-day newsroom – or the lack of it.

He was brought up in the days when the constant noise of stressed reporters hammering away at their typewriter keys was enough to induce hearing damage. Add to that the cloying smell of cheap cigarettes smoked one after the other by journalists desperate to meet a deadline and you had an unhealthy workplace. Yet Cooper preferred the old way.

Now, post-Covid, when traditional ways of working in some industries had changed, many of his staff worked from home. Newspaper executives under constant financial pressures realised that journalists needed only a good wi-fi connection to file their stories. So the bosses didn't renew the lease on their offices.

Cooper also missed the sound of a newsroom. The more noise the better for Cooper whose productivity increased incrementally.

Reporters still had to go out to cover court cases and meet contacts. But otherwise there was little need for journalists to venture into the office. Unless, like today, they were being given a pep talk.

The news editor was about to get to his feet when he grabbed his nose and screwed up his eyes.

'Shit! What's that smell?'

No one answered.

'Did somebody come back from a job last night with a curry and decided to save some for breakfast? It's bloody vile!'

Again, silence.

'Can't you smell it, Tony?'

'Sorry, Bill, no. Haven't been able to get a whiff of anything since I had Covid,' Tony Goodson replied.

'Someone fetch the cleaner. Tell her to empty the bins and spray something to get rid of the stench.'

Cooper composed himself and stood up, his shoulders drooping from an accumulation of years hunched over typewriters and laptops. He pushed his floppy, dark hair off his forehead and called the meeting to order.

'Good to see you all again in person – much better than a Zoom call or having to speak to you on the phone. Mind you, some of you look even worse than I remember!'

There were stifled laughs around the room.

'First of all, an announcement. Our chief reporter Tony Goodson has been nominated for reporter of the year in the Regional Press Awards. Well done, Tony, you deserve it.

'Now, Tony's up against some stiff competition from reporters on Scotland on Sunday, the Belfast Telegraph and WalesOnline. But I'm confident he'll pull it off. He's come up with several cracking lead stories recently and I'm sure none of the other journalists has been as prolific as our Tony. Take today's paper, for instance.'

He held up that day's edition of the East Midlands Express, the only newspaper still surviving in the region whose circulation was dropping by the week.

'Here we have a brilliant human-interest story written by Tony. Let him tell you all about it.'

Goodson rose steadily, trying to look embarrassed but failing to hide a self-satisfied look which engulfed his face.

In his early forties, he'd experienced what veteran journalists described as the good old days. But he'd grasped the latest technologies and used them to ensure he didn't let any of the younger, ambitious staff take advantage of him.

He stretched to his full height, his dark, regularly cut hair, smart suit, button-down shirt and bright tie giving him the aura of an accountant or a solicitor rather than a journalist.

'I'm not one to blow my own trumpet,' he began, causing a couple of the senior reporters to snigger. 'I think Bill wants me to address the youngsters among you particularly. You only worked in a modern newsroom for a short time and now you're spending a lot of time working from home.'

He couldn't resist a dig at the management for what he felt was a short-sighted view of the industry: 'You spend a lot of your time making sure your stories are right for our online readers, ensuring enough people click on them, and we use far too much material that's syndicated. So a lot of you might not have been through what's known in the business as the "death knock".'

It was one of the jobs that most journalists feared: turning up unannounced at the home of a bereaved family trying to find out more about the person who'd died. Yet despite this being a frequent occurrence, most news organisations gave their employees neither training nor guidance about how to approach grieving relatives.

'This was a really sad case,' Goodson continued. 'Helen Loudon's six-week-old son Jack was admitted to hospital with a virus. But the staff didn't monitor his condition closely enough. He suffered brain damage and died. Everyone, radio, television, national papers, wanted the story but I was the one who got it.

'You can imagine how distraught his mother was. So it didn't help when a reporter and a camera crew from a TV station – admittedly they were working to a deadline – tried to bamboozle her into an interview. She was pissed off and told them where to go.

'I took my time before approaching her. I apologised for intruding. I said I was sorry for her loss and I couldn't imagine what she was going through. I treated her with dignity. And respect. Looked on her as a bereaved mother rather than someone who'd got a story to tell. The upshot was that after a while she agreed to be interviewed.'

He paused, ensuring that the whole room was taking in every word he said.

'So what was the next thing I did? The following day – and it was still the day before we intended running the story – I called her to make sure she was okay. Checked if she was happy for us to go to print. She was.

'I told her we'd contacted the hospital for a comment and they might not apologise because it was an ongoing case. I also said the story would go online as well as the printed edition. I mentioned that there might be a few adverse comments, not because people thought she should take a share of the blame for what happened to her son but because some idiots just do that – they post stuff on social media because they think the world needs to know their opinion.

'But after listening to me, Helen said she'd stay away from social media altogether. So there you are – that's how to get a great story.'

Goodson sat down, unable to disguise the pride and self-congratulation that were apparent on his face.

Cooper, full of admiration for his star reporter, jumped in.

'Tony, don't be so modest about your achievements. Tell us how you retained control of the interview and what's going to happen next.'

This time Goodson relaxed and remained seated. His facial expression didn't change.

'The aim is to give the interviewee a choice as to where you have your chat. We did it in Jack's bedroom – Helen thought she was taking charge but I controlled the whole thing. I listened and looked at her the whole time. She felt comfortable, safe.

'It's all about making a connection. I'm going to see Helen again later this morning. I've advised her to consider consulting lawyers about whether to take legal action. She's giving me the exclusive story – again.'

Simon Powell, an inquisitive, perceptive journalist in his mid-twenties, knew he should give Goodson credit for the story which would undoubtedly sell more papers. But there was something about Goodson which Powell found odd. He just couldn't put his finger on it.

Goodson picked up a copy of the Express which was on the desk next to him and admired his handiwork. He looked forward to his name being splashed across the front page on yet another occasion.

8

West showed his warrant card to the uniformed officer who was preventing anyone unauthorised from getting close to the crime scene. The officer lifted the blue-and-white tape, allowing West to approach the suitcase. The smell caused his nostrils to twitch.

He met the crime scene manager who told him what actions had been taken since the police had been called.

'We've cordoned off the street. A pathologist is on his way, we're getting a team to go house to house and we managed to stop the dustbin lorry going to the tip.

'I pity the poor buggers who'll have to dig through all that rubbish for clues. It's a shame we can't get some of the low life of Nottinghamshire to go through it as part of their community service. But they'd probably be looking for stuff to nick rather than any severed limbs.'

West didn't take in what the crime scene manager was suggesting because he was so focused on the investigation, thinking about all the basic tasks that needed to be carried out in what was known as the golden hour – the time when police had to protect the scene and recover as much evidence as possible. He was grateful that the first officers on the scene automatically knew what had to be done.

He looked around the street which hadn't seen so much activity since a party to celebrate the Queen's silver jubilee.

Any witnesses? CCTV? He almost forgot: the woman who lived in the house where the suitcase was found. Could she shed any light on how it came to be there or its contents?

He pressed the doorbell and waited. A family liaison officer greeted him and took him to meet Violet Campbell. She used a walking stick as she stood to welcome him; West was worried she might fall over before returning to her chair.

She took a deep breath as she sat, the exertion of getting up draining her of most of her strength. She often pushed her glasses back towards the bridge of her nose, West noticing they were so old they were almost falling apart.

Her skin was dry, discoloured and sagging while her teeth looked as though they'd had little attention for a number of years. She tried to manipulate her greying hair into place but it had a will of its own, requiring her regularly to brush strands out of her eyes and back behind her ears.

She beckoned West to sit on a settee which at one end was occupied by two immaculately groomed cats. She looks after them more than she looks after herself, West decided.

He assumed his most caring demeanour as he began questioning her.

'Is it Mrs Campbell?'

'Yes, dear, but I've been a widow for nearly twelve years now. You can call me Violet.'

'Thanks, Violet. Do you know anything about the suitcase that was found next to your dustbin?'

'No, dear, I've never seen it before.'

'You don't own a suitcase yourself?'

'Haven't had one since . . .' She looked up as she tried to recollect when it was – 'before my Eric passed away. We used to go on holiday together all the time. Well, at least twice a year. But I just couldn't face it after I lost him. A couple of years after he died I shoved all his clothes in our suitcase and gave it to a charity shop. Haven't been away since.'

A couple of minutes later West was under no misapprehension that Violet Campbell had nothing to do with the torso found on the pavement next to her dustbin.

He thanked her for their chat, left her house and headed back to Police HQ, a futuristic-looking building on the southern edge of the city.

Two hours passed, with West checking and re-checking every piece of evidence that had started to come in.

Anxiety almost turned to paranoia as he looked at everything yet again, almost convincing himself that he'd missed something.

He called the team together for a briefing. 'I want to make sure we've got all bases covered. Let's get a good start on this one.'

West began to relax, confident in the knowledge that if he'd overlooked anything, one of the team would spot it.

'Here's what we've got so far. Binmen from the local council found a suitcase this morning on a street in Aspley. It contained a torso; no arms, no legs and no head.

'First of all, we need to identify whose torso it is and find the other limbs.'

Tilly Johnson, no longer regarded as a newcomer after proving how capable she was in a couple of previous investigations, interjected.

'I'm onto that. The pathologist should be able to tell us the age of the torso – whether this is a relatively new crime or if it happened a long time ago and someone's only now decided to get rid of the body.'

West was in full flow: 'Just as important, we need to find out whether anyone saw the guy with the suitcase in that street. Admittedly it was late at night but there might be witnesses who can help identify him.'

West told the team about his visit to Violet Campbell's house and assured them she knew nothing about the suitcase.

He looked around, waiting for someone else to contribute. The room went silent before Paul Allen cleared his throat.

The joker among the team, Allen always had what he thought was a witty comment he had to share. His colleagues braced themselves – their expectations were well founded.

'Perhaps we should check for someone who's been shopping and spent a lot of money.'

Quizzical looks around the newsroom.

'The person's obviously bought something that cost them an arm and a leg!'

West gave him a solemn stare but thought he might be exceeding his position if he reprimanded Allen in front of his colleagues.

'Seriously, though,' said Allen, 'we've checked for CCTV but there's nothing on the street. It's an area that's suffered from small-time burglaries in the past, but people living there reckon they haven't got anything valuable, so they don't think it's worth installing cameras. We're widening the search to see whether anyone in the vicinity has got them.'

West resumed: 'Before the suitcase was moved the CSIs took swabs from the outside, the zips and the handles. They're hoping whoever put the body in the case will have left their DNA. I've asked for the results to be fast-tracked to us.

'I've got officers checking the streets for anything else – the victim might have left traces of blood which dripped out of the case. A murder weapon might have been discarded close by. We need to find out as much as we can about that suitcase. That could be a vital piece of evidence.'

West looked at his colleagues in turn, hoping that one of them would add something useful. When no one spoke he summed up the case himself.

'For all we know, the victim could have been killed accidentally. We might be looking at someone merely hiding the body and preventing a burial.

'But putting it in a suitcase and trying to get an old lady to take the rap – that's despicable. We need a result on this one as soon as we can.'

9

Helen Loudon finished dusting the lounge, then dragged her vacuum cleaner from a cupboard under the stairs and gave the carpet a quick once-over.

She dashed upstairs, checked her hair was in place and squirted herself with her favourite perfume.

It's only a reporter, she told herself as she made sure she wouldn't have looked out of place in one of the better restaurants in the area.

Forming relationships with the opposite sex had never been Helen's strong point. As a teenager she'd given in too easily to youths who were interested only in adding her name to their list of conquests.

In her twenties she frequented nightclubs and drank so much alcohol that she put up little resistance whenever anyone wanted to drive her home and decided to make a detour down a country lane.

She thought she'd turned a corner when she met a man who promised to care for her for the rest of her life. But shortly after she announced she was pregnant he disappeared. She never saw him again. He didn't even go to Jack's funeral.

After surprising herself with how well she coped on her own, she was determined not to get involved with a man again. Her girlfriends told her she was doing the right thing; the words 'men' and 'trust' just didn't go together, they warned. But she couldn't make her mind up whether they were telling the truth or were just saying the words they thought she wanted to hear. After all, several of those friends were now married and most seemed blissfully happy.

But then she met Tony. Was he different? He'd been gentle, respectful, helpful when he discussed what had happened to Jack. They built up a rapport. But was he doing it simply to get a story for his newspaper? She didn't think so.

She'd watched enough news programmes and documentaries on television to know that journalists could be cynical, selfish and immoral. Was Tony like that? Not on the surface.

The doorbell rang. She paused in front of the mirror, checked her appearance again and hoped her heart would stop thumping so uncontrollably.

Miles felt dreadful. He'd hardly slept because he was worrying about Daisy Higgins. He'd been wishing his phone would ring to relieve his anguish one way or the other – but it remained silent throughout the early hours.

He got up, his head pounding and his stomach gurgling as though he'd sunk enough alcohol to give him a stonking hangover. But he'd been careful with the amount he'd drunk.

Two cups of coffee and a shower as hot as he could bear virtually prepared him for work. A crisp, white shirt, a colourful tie and his most expensive aftershave lifted his mood as he set off for work.

James West was already at his desk when Miles arrived, the detective sergeant having a stern look on his face as he went through the previous day's papers about the torso in the suitcase.

'Good morning, James. What's going on? I take a day off and you're after my job!' Miles smiled, hoping his expression conveyed that he wasn't being serious.

'Not at all, boss. You weren't here and the detective superintendent needed a right-hand man. Couldn't believe he chose me.'

'Well, I don't suppose there was anyone else.' Miles paused, waiting for West's reaction before continuing.

'I'm joking. The DS made a good choice. If he'd asked me, I'd have put your name forward immediately.'

A joyous smile covered his face and Miles noticed a sense of relief in West's eyes.

'But I might have to change my mind if you've messed up on your first investigation.'

45

The smile disappeared to be replaced by concern as West checked through everything again.

'We've got a team going through the contents of the dustbin lorry to see if we can locate the missing limbs. Doubt if we'll find a murder weapon but you never know – we may get lucky.

'We've interviewed everyone at the scene including the binmen and the old lady at the house where the suitcase was found. We're trying to get hold of CCTV from the surrounding area. We've been looking to see if there's any footage from video doorbells – but it's not the sort of area where people have them.

'Obviously we can't get any fingerprints from the torso and we won't be able to make an identification through dental records. A Home Office pathologist is taking samples so that we can get DNA.

'The suitcase has been sent off for forensic examination. We're checking its age to see whether that'll give us any clues. We're also going through the missing persons' list. Once we've got DNA, we can check whether we've got an ID. If not, we'll have to go back further.'

'What about the missing limbs?'

'I've got Tilly looking into that. She's checking if there've been any reports of limbs found in the area recently.

And Paul's delving back to see if we've had any similar cases, solved or unsolved, or killers cutting up bodies.'

'Witnesses?'

'In hand. There's a team doing house-to-house.'

This time Miles was deep in thought. 'Aspley,' he said eventually. 'Has its fair share of unemployed people. They won't necessarily be in bed very early. Someone could have still been up and saw what was going on. Let's hope so.'

Miles looked stern. It was a good ten seconds before he spoke again.

'First-class job, James. You *will* be after my job at this rate.'

10

Tony Goodson walked up the short path past the well-trimmed lawn and carefully tended flowerbeds of Helen Loudon's semi-detached home.

With one hand he straightened his tie although he knew he looked smart and sophisticated. The other hand remained behind his back.

Helen heard the doorbell and, anxious not to seem too keen, walked slowly to the front of the house and checked again in a mirror that her hair was in place.

She opened the door and was surprised to see Goodson produce a bouquet.

'Oh, Tony, you shouldn't have.' A tear came to her eye. 'I can't remember the last time anyone bought me flowers.'

'You deserve them. Thought they might cheer you up a bit. Bring some colour to the place.'

He looked around the small yet meticulously clean lounge which appeared homely despite the ageing furniture. The arms on the sofa were beginning to fray and the coffee table had scuff marks on the legs and a circular stain caused by a hot drink.

He recognised the similarities between this home and the one he was brought up in. It was a loving, caring household. He wasn't conscious of it at the time but it too had outdated furnishings. However, that was due to his parents' unquenchable desire that Goodson should have the best possible education and later a profession which would make them proud.

When his father died from pancreatic cancer, Goodson reassessed what he wanted to do with his life. He didn't crave a mundane, mind-numbing job no matter how much money and status it might bring him.

His parents would have liked him to become a lawyer. Although he was interested in legal matters, he couldn't see any satisfaction in defending criminals who were clearly guilty or making a case for a defendant not to be sent to prison when his or her crime deserved a custodial sentence.

He began to take a passionate interest in current affairs, trying to understand why people in positions of authority made what were often unjustifiable decisions.

It was when he realised that as a journalist he could hold politicians and business leaders to account that he realised he'd found his ideal career path.

He gained a first-class honours degree in journalism, noticing that most of his fellow students at university had nowhere near his command of the English language. His confidence when talking to strangers, his adeptness at recognising good news stories and his ability to attract readers with his style of writing impressed bosses at a newspaper. A job offer followed as soon as he graduated.

As part of the job he spent plenty of time in court, reporting on the antics of criminals who were either too stupid or too ill-prepared to get away with their misdemeanours.

He took huge pride when a story appeared in print, his byline letting the world know that he was the journalist who'd revealed the complete, unsavoury details of the court case.

He paused for a moment and considered the kudos that would be heaped on him when Helen's medical negligence case came to court. He had no doubt whatsoever that she'd win and get a huge payout.

'How've you been?' he asked Helen, the sincerity in his voice putting her at ease.

'Fine. Just fine. Would you like tea?'

He knew she was putting on a show. Accepting her hospitality allowed Helen to retain a sense of control. He didn't want to do anything to antagonise her.

His phone pinged with a message. 'Sorry,' he said as he switched it to silent.

He followed her into a poky yet tidy kitchen where she filled the kettle and put tea bags into two mugs.

There was the hint of tension in the air which Goodson tried to quell.

'I simply don't know how I'd have coped with something similar to what you've been through. Do you think you're ready to take your case further?'

She looked at the kettle which seemed to be taking an inordinate amount of time to boil.

'I think so. If you'll help me.'

Goodson's gaze locked onto Helen's pleading eyes and didn't move.

'I've had an informal chat with a guy I know who works for a firm of solicitors specialising in medical negligence cases. They're good – they're experienced in all kinds of issues. It's only a small team but they've received the highest ranking available for their handling of cases over the past couple of years.

'They'll work on a no-win, no-fee basis if you decide you want them to represent you. My contact's told me you've got three years to start a claim, so you're well within that. But if you're going ahead, you need to move as soon as possible because they'll have to do some preliminary investigations – instructing medical experts and so on.

'He also told me that the case may be resolved without you having to go to court. What they call a pre-trial settlement. So let's hope that's what happens. We don't want you going through any more stress.'

Helen sighed, relief and relaxation engulfing her face as her worries ebbed away.

'Thanks so much. How come you know so many interesting people?'

Goodson shrugged, secretly enjoying the trust that was being built between them.

'Just part of the job. Whenever I meet anyone new, I make sure I get their contact details. You never know when they'll come in handy.'

'I simply don't know what I'd have done without you,' Helen gushed. 'I'd made some enquiries with legal firms but they were asking for thousands of pounds before they'd even look at Jack's case. I never even thought about someone taking it on on a no-win, no fee basis.'

'That's what I'm here for. It's always good to have a second pair of eyes coming at a situation from a different angle.'

Without warning Helen's mood changed and she tensed up. Goodson noticed immediately. 'What's wrong?'

'I'm concerned that people might get the wrong impression. I'm not doing it for the money.'

'Of course you're not. You want to prevent any other families having to suffer what you've been through since Jack's death. If you want, you can say you'll give any damages that the court awards you to a children's charity.'

Helen's anxiety subsided. He really is a decent man, she thought, as a trace of a smile reached up to her eyes.

Goodson smiled too although he was imagining the front-page headline when his story went to print.

11

Miles parked his car in the staff car park and hurried to the main entrance of police headquarters. Dense clouds that were as dark as a murky river seemed only feet above his head.

He went inside, asked the receptionist how she and her family were and used his key card to unlock the door to the areas the public rarely got to see.

He marched along the corridor and felt a pang of guilt as he noticed some of the younger members of the force working up a sweat in the luxuriously equipped gym.

He pushed open a door leading to the upper floors, preferring to get at least a small amount of exercise by taking the stairs two at a time. He stopped to pick up a copy of that day's East Midlands Express. A pile of papers was delivered every day although he had no idea why they weren't on display in reception.

After his dressing-down by the Chief Constable Miles made sure he got hold of a copy every day so that he wouldn't be in the dark if anyone at the Express criticised the force's performance.

He stopped short of the first stair and pressed the bell to call the lift so that he'd have more time to read the front-page article.

Tony Goodson's name was on the story with the bold headline **Murderers on the loose!** Miles speed-read the piece and when he got to his office went over it again, taking in every word:

Residents have expressed their concern after a record number of prisoners including convicted murderers absconded from an open prison.

People living in Sudbury, Derbyshire called a crisis meeting last night and demanded action from the Ministry of Justice.

They heard that more than 1,000 inmates had gone missing in the past twenty years from the Category D prison. Some had been sentenced to life for murder and were transferred to Sudbury towards the end of their sentence.

No fewer than ten are still on the run. One walked out four years ago and has yet to be found.

One irate resident told me: 'It's disgusting. I've got a wife and three young children. When I go out to work I want to know that my family is safe. But how can they be with all these prisoners on the streets? Murderers should serve their whole sentence behind bars. None of this rehabilitation rubbish — lock them up.'

Another told the Express: 'I was horrified when I learned that some of these prisoners who've been convicted of horrendous crimes are actually given jobs in the village. There's no guarantee they won't offend again. We're calling on the government to take action to keep these people out of our community.

'At the very least we want more police patrols around the village. We need to see a greater police presence.'

The local MP Theo Kennedy has added his voice to the controversy: 'I'm worried about how prisoners are chosen to be sent to Sudbury. Too many are absconding.

'These prisoners might be coming to the end of their sentence but there needs to be a more rigorous risk assessment.'

A spokesman for the Ministry of Justice commented: 'The vast majority of Sudbury inmates have shown great remorse for their crimes and want to integrate back into society.

'People abscond for lots of different reasons but mainly it's because a family crisis has developed or they've got a problem with a relationship. They're so wrapped up in their predicament that they don't think about the consequences of absconding – they'll end up back in a closed prison.

'We'll be meeting the residents of Sudbury to allay their fears and reassure them that those prisoners sent to Sudbury are chosen very carefully. They're not considered a danger to the public.'

The Express has contacted East Midlands Police for comment.

Miles was glad that the Sudbury problem wouldn't be landing on his desk – he already had enough to worry about.

He tried to concentrate on the torso investigation but couldn't help thinking about Daisy. By mid-morning he decided he couldn't carry on until he'd brought himself up to date with the previous night's events.

He called a uniformed inspector who'd been handed the case. He told Miles that Daisy's car had been found about a mile from her home but there was no sign of her. The car had been recovered and would at some stage be examined if the investigation escalated into anything more than a missing person inquiry.

He'd only just put the receiver down and was deep in thought when the phone rang, startling him.

The pathologist introduced himself and said he could announce his initial findings about the torso: 'It belongs to a female, early thirties who died recently, possibly in the past couple of weeks.

'Her organs are in relatively good order although it looks like she was undernourished. Whether that was her own doing or whether someone made sure she didn't get much food – well, of course, that's impossible for me to say. But her last meal was a greasy fry-up.

'There was also evidence of sexual activity. Again, impossible for me to tell whether that was consensual.

'The unfortunate thing, as far as you're concerned, is that she didn't have any identifying marks. So prevalent in young women these days – but she had no tattoos, no piercings.'

Miles ruminated over the pathologist's revelation before asking the crucial question: 'How did she die?'

The phone line went quiet. Miles was about to repeat the question when the pathologist sighed.

'Difficult to tell. No real signs of injury, so it's a bit of an odd one.'

'So, what are the alternatives?'

'Without the limbs, it's difficult to speculate. The femoral artery could have been punctured – a stab wound in the upper thigh, near the groin, could be fatal. Death could have occurred within a few minutes. That might be a reason for one of the legs being severed.

'Alternatively the young woman might have suffered a serious head injury and the perpetrator removed the head so that we couldn't establish what happened to her.'

'The limbs and the head,' said Miles. 'Would it have taken anyone with a good anatomical knowledge to remove them?'

'All you need is a knife to cut into the flesh and a saw to go through the bones. You don't have to be a surgeon to be able to do it. You could be looking for someone who's got medical experience. On the other hand, the person you're seeking might work in an abattoir. Or it could be someone who's picked up how to do it on the internet. I'm not trying to tell you how to do your job, inspector – but it's pretty vital that you find those limbs.'

12

The meeting room resembled a village hall or community centre where people might get together before a coffee morning or a flower-arranging class. Pastel colours on the walls, functional but barely comfortable furniture and thin, fraying carpet tiles proved that the organisation's meagre finances weren't frittered away on needless luxuries.

Helen, conservatively dressed in a white blouse and dark skirt, picked up a cup of tea and ignored the biscuits. She felt nervous, unsure of what she should do or say. Her awkwardness was evident in her eyes as well as her movements.

The hospital had advised grief counselling after Jack's death. She was dubious as to whether the sessions would help; how could hearing about other people's misfortune enable her to get over her loss? Talking about it with strangers was hardly likely to lift her mood, to give her the impetus to move on with her life. But she decided to take up the offer; no one could accuse her of not making an effort . .
.

The woman who stood next to Helen chomped on a digestive biscuit and slurped her tea. Making eye contact, she uttered: 'All right, duck?'

Helen nodded and forced herself to smile.

'Do you come here often?' said the woman, her gravelly voice the legacy of her smoking forty cigarettes a day since she was a teenager.

'Ooh, that sounds like a chat-up line! Blokes have said that to me a few times over the years. Didn't mean it that way.'

Wearing a pink hoodie and black joggers, the woman flicked her straggly, greying hair off her face and introduced herself.

'Monica Evans. You look a bit tense. Your first time here?'

Helen nodded and reached for a biscuit after all.

'They're not a bad bunch here. You should get on all right. If you don't you can always come and have a chat with me if you're feeling – you know, a little bit tearful.'

Helen found herself strangely at ease with this woman although they came from different backgrounds.

She began to relax as the room filled up and dared to ask what was really on her mind.

'Have you lost someone close, Monica?'

'Yeah. I suppose he was my boss but he was a real good friend. I didn't think they'd allow me to come at first, him not being a close relative and all that. But we're all in the same boat here.'

'Who was he then?' Any reservations Helen might have had about chatting to this new-found friend disappeared; she was fascinated to find out more.

'Guy called Ken Thompson. He was a great bloke. Really kind man. Always asking about our David, how he was getting on. Ken even paid for the grandson of someone I know to go to America for cancer treatment. Such a big heart, Ken.'

Helen's eyes showed not only a tenderness that made her look more attractive but also curiosity which drove her questioning.

'What happened to him?'

'Police shot him. Oh, I think he did a few dodgy things but the cops came after him, said he'd been murdering reporters and blew him away!'

Helen remembered reading about the case. She noticed that Monica's eyes had become moist. Ken had obviously meant a great deal to her.

'You poor thing. How on earth are you coping?'

'They say time's a great 'ealer. But it happened nearly a year ago. Not a day goes by without me thinking about 'im.'

She went quiet and composed herself.

'Sorry, duck, got wound up with my own problems. 'Ow about you? Why are you here?'

Helen told her how Jack's life had been cruelly taken away and explained how she would never get over the loss of her son. She told Monica about the pending legal action but maintained that no amount of money could compensate for Jack's death.

She began to choke and knew she had to think about something else.

'So what happened to the police who shot Ken?'

'Absolutely nothing. The case went to some watchdog group – can't remember what it's called – and they cleared those coppers. It was a bloody whitewash. There's no justice in the world – not for the likes of you and me at any rate.'

Helen put her hand on Monica's and smiled.

'There are other ways that you might be able to get justice. I think I know just the man who can help.'

13

James West could hardly contain his enthusiasm. 'Boss, the DNA results on the torso are in. We've got an ID. You won't believe who it is!'

'I won't unless you give me a clue. Pop star? Famous actress? Reality TV personality?'

'Remember that weather presenter off the telly who went missing – what, best part of a year ago? It's her!'

Felicity Strutt had disappeared after having a meal with her boss at a clandestine location. They were about to start a new life together in London – but she vanished and there'd been no sign of her anywhere.

At one stage the police thought she might have become another of crime boss Ken Thompson's victims, although that was ruled out when it was established Thompson had murdered journalists who'd written or broadcast inaccurate stories about his mother.

'Boss, here's what we've got on Felicity,' said West, handing Miles a file.

He quickly looked through it to reacquaint himself with the case.

After she and the television boss Chris Watson had left a hotel at different times, there was no record of what

Felicity did next or where she went. Her car was found abandoned; she'd not used her debit card or made any calls on her mobile.

'Right, first of all we need to tell her husband what's happened. We can't rule him out at this stage – I remember there was something odd about Rob Woodcock.

'Then we need to find out more about Felicity's lifestyle. What places did she frequent? What did she get up to when she wasn't at work? Who did she spend time with?

'And, most important of all, we need to find out who put the suitcase outside Violet Campbell's house. James, anything from CCTV?'

'Not yet, boss. There's not a lot of footage and what there is doesn't really give us any idea what happened.'

'Okay, any theories?'

Tilly Johnson got everyone's attention as soon as she spoke.

'Boss, I've done a check on whether any unidentified limbs have been found in the area over the past year. Nothing.

'So I've been doing some thinking. How much does a torso weigh? I've looked into it and it's just over fifty per cent of the weight of a person's whole body.

'Now, I'm no weightlifter but I still think it would be difficult for someone to carry that suitcase and walk any distance to Violet's. They'd probably need transport. Maybe not a car – the CCTV hasn't turned up any evidence of cars in the area at the time, so perhaps we need to check buses, see where the nearest bus stop is and find out if there's CCTV of anyone getting on with a suitcase. Possibly taxis too.'

'Good call, Tilly. You get onto the bus company. Check which buses were in the area on the night before the suitcase was found, when people were putting their bins out.

'Paul, grab a photograph of the suitcase and go round the local taxi firms, see if anyone with a heavy case booked a cab to anywhere near Violet's house.

'And James, check with the council. See if anyone's reported a strange smell in the area. It might be that for some reason, whoever did this to Felicity might not have preserved the body properly. If there was a bit of a stink, it could have forced the killer to get rid of the torso.'

Miles suddenly thought about Stuart Bainbridge's offer. He'd certainly miss the adrenalin-fuelled involvement of cases such as this. But then he remembered that Daisy Higgins had gone missing. Would she end up like Felicity?

14

It was a district of Nottingham that Miles knew by reputation rather than personal involvement. He'd investigated the occasional major crime in Aspley – an abusive husband who killed his wife in an uncontrollable rage, a spate of robberies when drinkers were threatened after leaving a pub – but it was an area that suffered from low-level crime more than anything else.

Burglaries were often high on the list of offences in Aspley along with drug seizures and anti-social behaviour by youngsters who had absolutely nothing to do in the evenings.

He appreciated that the police had brought in some initiatives as the nights were drawing in, warning locals to secure their shed although it had done little to reduce the number of thefts from gardens.

He also thought about how dedicated officers had tried to engage with secondary-school pupils by treating them as adults in a bid to stop them offending. It was a commendable idea but it didn't bring down the crime figures.

He recalled the days when he was a junior detective and a number of kids discovered the nearby Harvey Haddon Sports Centre. There they worked off their excess energy playing basketball. Miles had taken part in the odd game there himself in the days when he had more leisure time away from the demands of his job.

But everything changed in 2014. The city council ploughed sixteen million pounds into the complex and changed its name to a sports village. The authority wanted to attract international events and enhance Nottingham's position as "the home of sport".

A fifty-metre swimming pool and squash courts meant there was no room for basketball – the swish of a ball going through a hoop was heard no more.

But surely there had to be somewhere else where Miles could arrange a game for bored youngsters and keep them occupied?

He wondered what had happened to those budding superstars when they finally accepted they'd never be the next Michael Jordan or LeBron James. Had they turned to crime like many of their peers? The optimist in him hoped that somehow they'd keep up their interest in the sport and would stay on the right side of the law.

But would any of them be so callous as to chop up a body, stick the torso in a suitcase and try to put the blame on a dear old harmless woman?

He was hoping the CSI team would come up with some answers. And Tilly too. She was becoming an integral part of Davies' team and he was sure she'd discover CCTV which might identify whoever had dropped off the suitcase.

He realised he was relying on her much more – and not just in the office. As well as brainstorming ideas about criminal cases they were working on, she'd become a sounding board for him and he knew he could discuss absolutely anything with her.

'You're a detective – I reckon it's about time you examined the evidence in front of you. She's smitten.' Miles recalled what Daisy Higgins had said about Tilly on the day he went to buy the extra tickets for the Storm's game against Kingston.

What did Tilly really think about him? But, more importantly, what had happened to Daisy?

Tilly Johnson was a great believer that people should be allowed to play to their strengths. She knew that anyone given a job they were good at would more than likely give a hundred per cent for the whole time.

In her last job, with Norfolk Police, she'd witnessed exactly the opposite. Her boss there allocated jobs on a rota basis; his philosophy was that variety meant officers didn't get bored and took on each new task with enthusiasm.

But Tilly had seen how stressed some of her colleagues had become when they were given some of the more unsavoury tasks to carry out. She'd even known officers to call in sick if they got an inkling they'd be working on something they'd rather avoid.

So Tilly was relishing the thought of obtaining CCTV footage from the bus company to try to find the man with the suitcase. It would be the team's best chance of moving the investigation forward although she knew it might lead to frustration. That was a hazard of the job: so many outside factors could affect an inquiry, such as witnesses failing to come forward, victims refusing to testify and the Crown Prosecution Service ruling that evidence wasn't strong enough to take a case to court.

Tilly was also hoping this might give her an opportunity to impress her boss. She'd been immediately attracted to Miles and thought he felt the same about her. They'd had a few drinks and a couple of meals together, leaving her with a yearning to get closer to him. He just had to dismantle a barrier that appeared whenever their relationship was leading towards its next stage.

Perhaps things might progress if she found out who'd been responsible for the torso in the suitcase . . .

She had a good feeling that she'd be able to identify the mystery man. She'd called the manager of the bus company and didn't have to charm him to help her. Maybe he was taken in by her voice; she didn't think anything of it but on more than one occasion colleagues had remarked that they found it sexy, sultry, seductive.

The bus company boss had heard one of his drivers say a scruffy, odd-looking man had struggled to get a case onto a late-night service. Tilly got the manager to give her a copy of the footage from the Nottingham City Transport 77 service a couple of days earlier. She sealed it in an envelope and signed it, ready to give it to a specialist CCTV officer who'd be given the task of scrutinising it for anything unusual.

She'd checked the route beforehand, noting that the service started on Maid Marian Way in Nottingham – once described as 'the ugliest street in Europe'.

When she first arrived in the city Tilly did a tour of landmarks to familiarise herself with the surroundings. She didn't find anything she thought was especially ugly, although she felt she had to do more research when she came across the strangely named Sir John Borlase Warren pub. She learned that the hostelry on Canning Circus had been named after a nineteenth century war hero and she was determined to pay it a visit at some point to raise a glass to the Royal Navy admiral.

The 77 bus had left the city centre, travelling up Alfreton Road and Aspley Lane before ending its journey at Strelley. Violet Campbell's house was just off the route. Tilly smiled; she was optimistic the investigation was beginning to get somewhere.

15

Miles was deep in thought when his phone rang. He picked up the receiver and immediately recognised the frenetic, charged atmosphere that was always present in the control room.

He pictured the rows and rows of desks with operators facing a bank of screens, each in their own isolated world as they dealt with the huge number of calls that came in every minute.

He knew it wouldn't be just those taking emergency calls who'd be busy: there'd be the call handlers dealing with people reporting petty crimes which wouldn't be serious enough to be investigated; and there'd be switchboard operators just as there would be in any business employing hundreds of people.

He wondered how those operators were performing today. All police forces were judged on how quickly operators answered both emergency and non-emergency calls. The East Midlands Constabulary had a good record and was considered one of the most efficient in the country for getting resources where they were needed as fast as possible.

In his mind's eye Miles also saw the top desk with a chief inspector, control room inspector and sergeant, constantly watching the jobs as they came in and making sure that the force responded appropriately to each call.

'Hello, Miles.' Davies heard the control room inspector's gruff but friendly voice. 'I hear you were interested in a woman who went missing last night.'

'Have you found her?' The urgency and expectation in his question were unmistakeable.

'Sorry to disappoint you. We haven't located her but we've got her car. We've recovered it because it was causing an obstruction. On the road leading into Hilton.'

Miles knew the south Derbyshire village which had been growing so rapidly he felt it was only a matter of time before it was classified as a town. It was ideal for anyone working in Derby and people would also commute from there to Stoke or even Manchester.

'Appeared to have broken down. We've got it in the garage and we'll have a look at it later. No sign of the driver, though.'

'Perhaps someone gave her a lift. It's not a dodgy area, as far as I'm aware. In fact I hear it's a decent community. People often help each other out. Maybe someone didn't want her out on the street on her own late at night and gave her a lift.'

But why not take her home, Miles thought.

He thanked the control room inspector and asked to be kept up to date with developments.

Miles was aware that Daisy lived in Hilton. He wondered why she hadn't called her mum to tell her what had happened. There were still plenty of questions that needed to be answered.

It didn't take long for the CCTV officer to find exactly what Tilly was looking for: a scruffy man in a tatty overcoat struggling to get on a bus with a heavy suitcase. He had a short conversation with the driver before sitting down near the front, not wanting to exert himself more than he needed to. A few stops later he got off.

Tilly was also shown footage of the last bus going in the opposite direction. The same man got on without his case; he stayed on for only a short time. She felt like jumping for joy. But she had a setback when the bus company boss told her the 77 bus had been thoroughly cleaned since that evening, reducing the chance of finding DNA on the seat.

Despite that, she remained hopeful of finding out who the man was. Surely someone in the area knew him. She'd do a check with the local beat team and also find out if there were houses with CCTV anywhere near the bus stop where the man got off.

She also arranged for the bus driver to drop into the police station once he'd finished his early shift.

Greg Butler was a former NCT driver of the year. He'd been recognised for being a great role model, talking to every passenger who got onto his bus and sincerely wishing them a nice day as they left.

In his mid-forties, he had a full head of dark, healthy hair but his face lacked colour and his waist was beginning to hang over his trousers – problems of spending too much time behind the wheel and getting little exercise.

He told Tilly he recalled the man with the case who was a regular on the 77.

'I don't know much about him. I only know him as Billy.

'Sometimes he wants to have a chat. At other times it's difficult to get a word out of him. Like the night in question. When I said "good evening" he just grunted. I mentioned that it was quite late for him to be out but he didn't make any reply. Couldn't wait to sit down. Usually goes upstairs. But that night he sat down right behind me.'

'Did he say anything about the suitcase?'

'No. I tried to strike up a conversation and asked him if he was going on holiday. He just said no. Then I managed to get another look at the case. It was really old – they don't make 'em like that any more.'

'Any idea where he lives?'

Butler took a sip of water from the cup on the table in front of him.

'He can't live too far from the bus stop. I picked him up one day when it was raining quite heavily. He wasn't wearing a coat but he was hardly wet, so I guessed he hadn't come very far. He was only on the bus for a couple of stops before he got off again.'

Tilly continued her questioning, finding out that the man with the case never travelled with anyone else, always dressed in dark, shapeless clothes and occasionally gave off an odour that indicated it was a while since he'd had a bath or a shower.

'Any idea what he did for a living?'

Butler thought for a moment before recalling a journey when the man was unusually talkative.

'He was laughing a bit as he spoke – I think he'd had a few beers. Quite unlike him.

'He said he'd had all sorts of jobs but didn't stay in any of them for very long. It was definitely the drink talking – he was trying to crack jokes but they just weren't funny. I remember once he said he wanted to be a doctor but didn't have the patience. He laughed but I didn't.

'One thing stuck in my mind: he said there was a job he really enjoyed but he had a horrible boss who made his life hell. He was fired because he threatened his boss with a meat cleaver. So that was the end of his career as a butcher.'

16

Miles hosted the early-evening briefing and was anxious to tie up as many loose ends as possible before letting his team go home for some much-needed rest.

James West told everyone that Felicity Strutt's husband was going to be questioned about her disappearance. He'd been ruled out during the initial investigation – but many victims were murdered by people they knew, so it was thought appropriate to have another word with him.

West had also checked the whereabouts of television boss Chris Watson. He'd told police he and Felicity had had an affair and were moving to London to new jobs and a new life together. He was believed to be one of the last people who saw Felicity. Someone would speak to him again.

As for a murder weapon on the streets near where the suitcase had been left: uniformed officers had made a painstaking search of the area but found nothing.

Paul Allen told the meeting that incidents of murderers cutting up their victims' bodies were rare: 'There was a case in Nottingham back in 1999 – Simon Charles, throttled his flatmate and chopped his corpse up into 12 pieces. He put them into bin bags and dumped them in a cemetery behind his home. Did it because his friend was annoying him.

'Said he got his inspiration from Dennis Nilsen, the serial killer. Charles is serving life, so we haven't got to worry about him.

'There was a case in Chesterfield a couple of years ago. Daniel Walsh murdered his landlord, cut off his head and arms and put them down a badger sett. He was going to clear off to France but he was arrested beforehand. Got sent down for twenty-seven years. Another one who we can rule out.'

Allen explained he'd also been talking to the council about unusual smells. 'My inquiry caused a bit of a stink but there's been no whiff of anything untoward.'

He ignored the groans and said none of the drivers with local taxi companies had reported seeing a man struggling with a heavy case.

Tilly was eager to share what she'd found out, starting with the suitcase.

'It was made by a company that went out of business years ago. When it first came out, early 1960s, it was supposed to be the cheapest and simplest on the market.

'It's got scuffs and surface marks – but they just show it was made a long time ago. The hinges are rusty. It's like something you'd see on that TV programme – *Antiques Road Trip*. It'd be classed as retro today, but it just looks ancient to me,' she said as she pointed to a picture of the suitcase on one of the white boards at one end of the room.

'My granny had one like that,' a detective constable gushed. 'So did mine,' said another. 'We found all sorts of things in it when she died and we cleared out the house – clothes, old curtains, even a couple of special editions of newspapers.'

'My granny was a right hoarder,' proclaimed the first detective. 'I can't believe – '

'Hey, guys, let's focus on the investigation.' There was the faintest hint of annoyance in Miles' voice. 'Anything else, Tilly?'

She told the team about her conversation with Greg Butler. She also handed out photographs taken from CCTV of their new prime suspect: the man known only as Billy. Uniformed officers would be on the streets of Aspley the following morning trying to identify him.

'Good work, everyone,' said Miles with heartfelt sincerity. 'Looks like tomorrow's going to be another busy day.'

Tony Goodson smiled as he picked up the day's first – and only – edition of the East Midlands Express. He recalled a time when there would be two or even three editions a day, allowing newspapers to change the front page completely if a new, sufficiently juicy story broke.

No matter. Everyone who saw the Express that day would see Goodson's name prominently displayed along with one of his favourite words: exclusive.

'Bereaved mum to sue hospital' screamed the headline. The story detailed how Helen Loudon was taking action against the hospital where her son died. There was a picture of her shedding tears as she told Goodson she didn't really want to punish hospital staff who like everyone in the NHS was under so much pressure – but she was determined that no one else should suffer the agony, devastation and heartbreak she'd been through.

He rang Helen, the newspaper being displayed in the centre of his spotlessly tidy desk for everyone to see.

'It looks really good. I'll get a copy sent round to you. I'm positive that everyone will be on your side when they find out how the hospital failed Jack.'

Helen was gushing in her thanks. 'How can I ever repay you? You've done so much already.'

82

'That's okay. Don't think I'm going to abandon you now that you've given me the story. I'll be with you every step of the way – all the way to court, if necessary. But I don't think it'll get that far. I'd be willing to bet that the hospital will offer to settle fairly quickly.'

Tears dripped onto Helen's cheeks. She couldn't decide if they were tears of relief or happiness.

'I'm forever in your debt. You've been so good to me.'

'Just my way of trying to make the world a better place.'

'Maybe. But what can I do for you? How about I cook you dinner for a start?'

17

It didn't take long for officers to put a name to the man with the suitcase: Billy Phillips was a familiar face in Aspley – and few people seemed to speak highly of him.

'He's a bit creepy. I don't go anywhere near him. You never know what he might do to you,' one resident said.

Another offered: 'I reckon he's got mental health problems. Saw him one day brandishing what appeared to be a rifle. Turned out to be a kid's toy. But it really put the wind up me. Good job I'm not of a nervous disposition – I could have had a heart attack.'

Davies wondered why that person hadn't reported the fact that someone was on the streets with an imitation firearm. It could have led to Phillips' being brought to their attention much earlier.

Paul Allen found Phillips' address by looking on the electoral roll. Neighbours confirmed where Phillips lived and the team sprang into action.

A check on the force's crime recording system revealed Phillips had convictions which had begun three years previously with stealing women's clothing from a washing line. He'd also been before the courts for exposing himself and his most recent appearance was for sexual assault during which he fondled the buttocks of a woman on a crowded bus. He was given a 12-month community order and was put on the Sex Offenders' Register for five years.

'We've got enough evidence to hold him on suspicion of murder,' asserted Davies. 'CSIs can go through his house and see if there are any clues to what he's done with the rest of Felicity.'

Davies drank the last of his coffee which was almost cold. His phone rang. He grabbed it, hoping to deal with the interruption as quickly as possible.

'Hello, Miles. Sorry, I've got some really bad news for you.' The control room inspector sounded nervous and full of trouble.

'We've got reports of a body being found in a brook. Out at Hilton. We haven't got a positive ID yet but we think it's your friend Daisy Higgins.'

Davies' legs almost gave way and he slumped into his chair.

'How can you be sure?'

'We found her Derby Storm ID pass in her pocket.'

18

Detective Superintendent Tom Brooksby was in his office when Miles tapped on the door and waited to be called in. Normally Miles was upbeat but Brooksby noticed the DI's shoulders were hunched and a frown was so prominent as to be unmistakeable.

'Have a seat, Miles. What's up?'

He told Brooksby about the body presumed to be that of Daisy Higgins and his concern for both her mum Christine and her son Joey.

'I suppose you want to take a look at the case, see what you can do. It's a cliché but I suppose you want justice for her.'

'And for her family. I'd like to go to Hilton as soon as possible.'

'Where are we with the Felicity Strutt case?'

'Suspect identified. We're going to stake out his house – from a distance, of course – so that we don't spook him, and probably lift him first thing in the morning.'

'Good work. Sounds as though you're on top of everything. I tell you what: James West can look after the arrest. You take over the Daisy investigation for the time being until I can assign another DI to it.'

'Thanks. Oh, I may need someone to give me a hand in the initial stages.'

'I know just the person. She's done a great job on the torso case. Take Tilly with you.'

The South Derbyshire village of Hilton which was mentioned in the Domesday Book in 1086 had grown enormously since houses were built on the site of a former Ministry of Defence depot. It was estimated that more than eight-and-a-half thousand people lived there; it was a desirable place to live because of its wide range of amenities, community spirit and low crime rate.

There was little to indicate it was the birthplace of a war hero: Air Commodore Herbert Martin Massey, the senior British officer at Stalag Luft III, the prisoner-of-war camp in World War II, authorised what became known as the Great Escape. A blue plaque was all that commemorated his life.

Miles and Tilly pulled up at the entrance to the village which was sealed off, a police car blocking everyone's way and a uniformed officer standing bolt upright in front of blue-and-white incident tape.

Miles showed his warrant card to the officer who was about to let him pass when an angry resident rushed up to them.

'Are you in charge?' he roared.

'I'm Detective Inspector Miles Davies. Can I help you?'

Despite the cold evening and the threat of more rain which had already soaked the pavements, the tall man with a bit of a paunch wore a tight, short-sleeved shirt. Several tattoos were visible including a skull, what Miles assumed were the names and dates of birth of the man's children and strange hieroglyphics which Miles found indecipherable.

'What the hell's going on? The whole bloody village seems to be cut off. I need to get home. My wife and kids are waiting for me. The kids are desperate to see me before they go to bed.'

'I'm sorry about that, sir, but this is a crime scene. No one's being allowed through at the moment.'

'But you can't just completely shut a place without giving us any warning. People have got things to do, places to go.'

Miles thought he'd seen virtually everything in his varied, incident-packed career but he never ceased to be amazed at the public's intransigence when it came to being forced to change their routine. Maybe in future criminals ought to post their intention to commit a crime on social media.

'Sir, I must reiterate that we believe a serious crime has been committed here. We need to gather as much evidence as possible from the scene which could be crucial to our investigation. And until we've done that, we can't allow anyone inside the cordon.'

Especially idiots like you, Miles thought but decided he'd said enough.

Tilly jumped in: 'We appreciate how inconvenient this is for you. I tell you what, sir, why don't you call your wife and tell her you're safe? You know how rumours can spread and she might be worried about you. In the meantime, we'll find out what's going on and see whether we can get you home before too long.'

The man inched away, chuntering to himself and muttering a few expletives that Miles thought were directed at the police generally, not him personally.

'Thanks, Tilly. You handled him a bit better than I did.'

'No worries, boss. I could tell immediately the sort of man he is. Won't be told in as many words what to do by a woman but manage his ego a bit and he'll do exactly what you want. He won't admit that a woman can boss him around – you just have to know how to handle him.'

They walked to a bridge over Hilton Brook where the speed limit changes from 30 to 40 miles per hour. The wind had blown most of the leaves off the trees, their branches bending over the water but giving neither shade nor cover.

A uniformed sergeant greeted them.

'Sir, the body was discovered by a passer-by. Going for a drink in one of the village pubs. Saw what he thought in the half light was something that had been thrown away. He's a bit of an environmentalist, helps out with litter picking. It's a community event held every so often. He was thinking that whoever dumped the rubbish was irresponsible. But then he had another look and realised it was a body.'

Miles peered into the water. Painful memories came back to haunt him. He couldn't help recalling two cases featuring children which had deeply affected him during his time as a police officer.

The first involved a four-year-old boy who'd drowned in a pond in his garden. His parents had left him unattended for only a short time – but it was long enough for the boy to overreach as he was trying to retrieve a football, fall in and fail to get out. Miles had been called to the house as part of the investigating team and felt so grateful that nothing similar had happened to his son Jordan when he was the same age as the dead boy.

The second case was more horrifying. When Miles was a detective sergeant he came across a nine-year-old boy who was in hospital after taking in more than five pints of water over a short period. It transpired that the boy's abusive father had tortured him by holding him down, covering his face with a cloth and pouring water over the boy's mouth to create a sensation of drowning. There were also fifty marks on the boy's body – evidence of physical abuse.

His father was sentenced to fourteen years in prison for causing grievous bodily harm. The only justification that anyone concerned with the case could come up with was that the father was, quite simply, evil and couldn't control his primeval urge to inflict pain.

Miles had never come to terms with his fear of water. When he was a boy some so-called friends had thrown him into the deep end at his local swimming pool. They remarked that it was the quickest way to teach a non-swimmer how to survive and he'd soon be as confident as an Olympic swimmer in the water.

The fact that a lifeguard had to fish him out because he was thrashing wildly and getting nowhere led to Miles' deciding never to go to a pool again.

Most of all, he hated the fact that he couldn't swim whenever he spent a day with Jordan. The youngster had been introduced to water at a very early age and often wanted to go to a pool. Miles was running out of excuses why they had to do something else instead.

'Boss, there's something you should know. The team are fairly certain it *is* Daisy,' Tilly said. 'But it's worse than we thought.'

She paused, hoping the couple of seconds' silence would be enough for Miles to brace himself for the horrific revelation: 'Daisy's had all her fingers chopped off.'

19

While the pathologist was preparing for Daisy Higgins' post-mortem examination, a CSI team was checking Hilton Brook for clues to establish whether she died where she was found or if her body had been carried by the current.

Miles and Tilly thought they'd done as much as possible and headed towards Nottingham. Tilly was surprised when Miles didn't take the A50, the Derby southern bypass, but stayed on the A516.

About three miles further on he pulled off towards Mickleover, a suburb of Derby which had retained its friendly feel despite rapid expansion due to several major housing developments.

Miles drove towards the centre, then turned into The Square which had just a few business premises including three estate agents almost side by side. He continued until he came to a car park behind the Masons Arms, a community pub with a history dating back to the seventeenth century.

They parked and walked quickly towards the back door as drizzle started to fall. Miles tapped the car's registration number into a tablet computer on the bar so that he didn't get a parking ticket. He ordered a pint of Bass for himself and a white wine for Tilly before sitting down next to her.

Miles had been to the Masons a couple of times before. He liked the quirky, split-level interior of the pub as well as its welcoming atmosphere.

From where they were sitting Miles could just make out a framed 1946 FA Cup final programme when Derby County beat Charlton Athletic 4-1 after extra time. It was the only time the Rams had won the competition.

He moved to take a closer look and chuckled to himself when he saw that Derby had played in what were described as white shirts and black knickers while Charlton wore red jerseys and white knickers.

He skimmed through the names of the players, many of whom had become folk heroes in the eyes of Rams' supporters: Leon Leuty, Reg Harrison, Horatio 'Raich' Carter, Jack Stamps and Douglas 'Dally' Duncan. What the fans would give to experience those glory days again . . .

Normally Miles frowned on staff who drank while on duty but these were exceptional circumstances. He'd known Daisy for several years and they'd grown close although there was never any romantic involvement.

Miles' son Jordan and Daisy's boy Joey mixed together at school and Miles had no idea how he was going to break the news to Jordan that he'd never see 'auntie' Daisy again.

'She was a good friend, wasn't she?' Tilly's voice was full of tenderness as well as concern for Miles.

'I only met her a few times at Storm basketball games but she came across as kind, considerate. She had so much love for Joey.'

'And her mum Christine. She'll be distraught too. They were such a close family.'

'What'll happen to Joey?'

'Not sure. I suppose the ideal situation would be for Christine to look after him. He's lost his mother; it wouldn't be good for him to be taken away from his grandma too.'

Tilly took a sip of her white wine, placed it back on the mat in front of her and considered the possibilities.

'What about Joey's dad? Will he try to get custody?'

'I would doubt it. As long as I've known Daisy, he's never been around. She didn't talk about him. Seemed he played no part in either Daisy's or Joey's life. If he turned up now he wouldn't have a very strong case – he might get access but I reckon custody would be out of the question.'

Tilly drank some more and ignored a couple of regulars who were greeted noisily when they entered the pub.

'Have you thought why the DS decided that you should take on this investigation? After all, you'd already got plenty on with the torso in the suitcase.'

'Brooksby was kept informed of what was happening in Daisy's case. He was aware that we were friends, so he probably thought I'd know about her lifestyle, habits, associates. That would give us a head start trying to track down her killer.'

'That sounds a good enough reason. Reckon he thinks the cases are linked?'

Miles was about to finish his pint but stopped. He waited until a couple who'd just come into the pub were out of earshot.

'Brooksby's a good cop. Came through the ranks the traditional way and knows what he's doing. I'm sure he thinks it highly unlikely that the guy who dissected Felicity Strutt also murdered Daisy. But I suppose he's keeping an open mind.

'Let's concentrate on Daisy for a minute. Someone kills her, then dumps her in a brook after cutting off her fingers. What does that tell us?'

Tilly replied immediately: 'Water can destroy DNA – or so some criminals think. Depends whether the water is contaminated with chemicals or pollutants and how long a body's been in the water.

"There might have been a struggle and the murderer's DNA could be under Daisy's fingernails. Removing them might prevent us identifying Daisy's killer. Sounds to me as though he – or she – is aware of forensics and will do everything possible to stay under the radar.'

Miles looked at the floor. He took what appeared to be an age before he spoke again.

'Why would someone want to kill Daisy? We need to find a motive. And one other thing we need to consider: where are Daisy's fingers now? Has the killer simply thrown them away – or is he keeping them as a trophy?'

20

Detective Constables Mark Roberts and Paul Allen didn't mind the early-morning start: potentially one of the most inhuman criminals they'd ever come across was about to be arrested. They were keeping watch on his house until the rest of the team arrived.

They pondered what the man who they believed had murdered Felicity Strutt and chopped up her body looked like. Would he be like Denis Nilsen, the Scottish serial killer who massacred at least twelve young men and boys before dismembering their bodies in the 1980s? What had been going through the mind of the callous killer who'd put Felicity's body in a suitcase and left it outside the home of a dear old lady, assuming she would get the blame?

Roberts had learned that appearances could deceive. People who seemed as though they might attack you if you looked at them in a strange way could demonstrate a genuine Christian attitude. On the other hand, there were those who were trustworthy on the surface but would metaphorically give you a good stabbing once your back was turned.

Roberts, dependable and one of the first to volunteer for anything that his colleagues might shirk from, sat in the driver's seat of their unmarked car with a coffee he'd made hours earlier, the thermal mug he'd bought from one of the major supermarkets keeping it at a drinkable temperature.

It was a grim start to the day as thick, grey clouds were beginning to open, depositing drops of rain and threatening a downpour.

They passed the time chatting about the pressures of the job, how wanting to get criminals off the streets had influenced their choice of career and how the job put almost unbearable pressure on their private lives.

'Have you ever been a victim of crime?' Roberts asked.

'Yeah, happened to me not long ago. I was on the forecourt of a petrol station at the time. I've obviously come across people who've suffered a similar ordeal but I never expected to feel the way I did when I was mugged. My hands were shaking, I went dizzy, I must have been in shock. Then I realised all my money had gone.

'Someone at the garage noticed what had happened. They must have dialled three nines. A uniformed guy came along. He was great – called for an ambulance because my blood pressure was through the roof.

'He asked me if I knew who did it. I told him it was pump number six!'

Allen went quiet. Roberts looked at him almost in disbelief. Then: 'Shit! You had me going there. I should have known you weren't being serious.'

'I've caught a few people out with that one.'

'What do you do, stay up all night trying to find jokes so you've always got one for any occasion?'

'There are a few things I subscribe to on Facebook, get some good gags there. People drop me a text or an email if they've got something they think I might be able to use. I've got a bit of a reputation to keep up, you know.'

Roberts was thinking of a way to get his own back, one that might finally shut up Allen. It would certainly get the backing of everyone at the station who'd suffered from Allen's sometimes banal attempts at being funny.

'Paul, what's the thing you fear most? What brings you out in sweat at the mere thought of it?'

'Public speaking,' replied Allen without pausing. 'I can tell a joke to a few colleagues or mates in the pub, but getting on my feet and having to address strangers – what a nightmare. I was best man at my brother's wedding a couple of years ago and of course I had to make a speech. Hated it. What a disaster. Throat tightened up, mouth went dry – and that was in front of a lot of people I knew.

'I've got so much respect for professional speakers – you know, those who can earn thousands of pounds for half an hour's work or whatever. And stand-up comedians. Some of the best like Peter Kay and Michael McIntyre can earn up to twenty million quid from doing one tour. They're welcome to it. No chance that I could do that.'

A plan was beginning to form in Roberts' brain.

More rain had fallen in the past couple of minutes and the sun hadn't even tried to break through the gloom. But as Roberts cast a glance out of the windscreen he could still make out what was going on outside.

Blue lights flashed, catching the attention of anyone who was out at that early hour. But sirens were switched off; police didn't want to announce their arrival.

A firearms team lined up on an order from their commander, hoping their expertise wouldn't be required although they were prepared for any eventuality. Behind them CSIs were donning white oversuits and overshoes, their white vans parked as close as possible to Phillips' house.

With everyone in place, an officer propelled his Enforcer, the official name for a red battering ram, at the front door. There was a low, ominous thud before a second swipe ensured that the door flew open. Shouts of 'armed police!' filled the street; tension and a sense of fear grew.

A few minutes later the suspect, wearing an oversuit and whose hands were cuffed behind him, was led out of the house and put in a van which had been sterilised before it left the station.

As the van headed off for the custody suite Roberts watched as the CSIs prepared to go in and sift through the house for the evidence that would be enough to convict Phillips of murder. Roberts knew they'd seize Phillips' clothes, bedding and anything that might have been used to carve up Felicity. They'd also check for her blood and see if Phillips had kept her limbs.

Be fascinating to see what they uncovered, Roberts thought.

21

Tony Goodson met Helen Loudon and Monica Evans in a coffee shop owned by one of the big chains. It looked like any other of the group's premises in any other town or city in the UK.

It was populated by students, some beavering away with an anxious look on their face and desperately trying to finish work which needed to be handed in shortly. Others seemed more laid-back, probably watching something banal on YouTube or checking out the latest proclamations from social media influencers, Goodson thought.

He marvelled that most of the students were drinking the most expensive coffees as well as eating overpriced paninis or snacks. He was baffled how they could afford such luxuries along with their tuition fees and rental accommodation.

Monica's rasping cough, the legacy of her smoking habit, caught Goodson's attention. It also alerted her presence to everyone else in the coffee shop.

Her grey hair, touching her shoulders and needing a thorough wash, occasionally covered one eye and forced her to shake her head so that she could see properly. Her blue puffa jacket which had a slight rip on one of her shoulders didn't look a though it would give her any warmth during the severely cold days ahead.

Goodson took their orders, Helen settling for a skinny latte but nothing to eat.

'Monica, what can I get you, cappuccino, americano, flat white?'

'Nah, none of that posh rubbish. I'll have a cup of tea.'

They managed to find a corner table that didn't have students or anyone else sitting close enough to hear their conversation.

Goodson thought how attractive Helen looked. The grief which had consumed her seemed to be ebbing away and her smile, although somewhat reserved, lit up her face.

'Monica, Tony's a reporter for the East Midlands Express. Now don't let that worry you – he's been brilliant helping me to take action against the hospital for Jack's death. I'm sure he'll be able to help you too.'

Monica looked nervous, unsure about the stranger even though he seemed at first sight a kind man. What did her father, whose name had appeared in newspapers after he'd been in court for committing petty offences, say about journalists? 'Wouldn't trust them as far as I could kick 'em.'

Helen explained how Goodson had found a firm of solicitors to take on her case and he might be able to do the same for Monica.

'How can I help? Tell me all about it.' Goodson's tone sounded reassuring.

Monica recounted how Ken Thompson, a legend on the estate where she lived, had looked after her and given her a job as his cleaner. He was a really generous man, she pointed out, and told Goodson how he'd paid for the grandson of a friend of hers to go to the United States for specialist cancer treatment that wasn't available on the NHS. Thompson had paid for flights and hotels as well as the expensive hospital bills. The boy, Ethan, was now growing up to be healthy and happy.

Goodson had followed the story about how Thompson had met his demise. He knew that the IOPC had conducted an investigation and all the officers had been cleared. So why was Monica not prepared to let Ken rest in peace?

'He was such a great bloke. Why did the police have to shoot him? Don't they have – what do they call them? Negotiators – who could have had a chat with Ken, got him to put his gun down, anything. I'll believe to my dying day that the police got it wrong.'

Goodson smiled. He wasn't thinking how good it would be to help Monica – he was imagining yet another front-page exclusive.

'I've been doing some research,' he said. 'I'm not a lawyer but I think you've got a pretty good case for taking civil action against the police.'

'What does that involve? I've got no money – 'aven't had a job since Ken died. I can 'ardly afford to buy food for me family each week.'

'Don't worry. There's a group of solicitors I know who'll look at your case. If your claim's successful they'll charge you a percentage of the compensation you'll get. It must have been a really frightening experience for you. You could press for damages for post-traumatic stress disorder, maintain that the police used excessive force when they shot Ken.'

Monica looked bewildered. 'Isn't that something soldiers get?'

'Yes, it is. But doctors have realised that it doesn't just happen to war veterans. Anyone can suffer PTSD if they go through a traumatic event. Sorry to intrude, but I need to ask you a couple of personal questions: do you suffer any flashbacks relating to the incident when Ken died?'

'Definitely.' The promptness of her reply took Goodson by surprise. 'I can be in the kitchen or cleanin' the living room and suddenly I'll have to stop because I can see it again – exactly what 'appened.'

'What about nightmares?'

'Nearly every night. I wake up covered in sweat.'

'Do you blame yourself for what happened to Ken?'

'I know I shouldn't but I can't 'elp it. Every time I 'ave one of those flashbacks I imagine what I could have done differently. I try to tell meself it wasn't my fault – but there's somefin' that stops me believing it.'

'And has anything got better with time?'

Monica drained her tea and wiped her mouth with her sleeve.

'It's got worse. I can't watch anyfin' on the telly where police 'ave got guns. I can't even watch an old cowboy film without it all coming back.'

Goodson's aura of assurance was at its maximum. 'Monica, it sounds as though you have a very strong case against the police. They did you wrong. They're going to pay for it.'

22

Tom Brooksby took his mug of coffee into the conference room, a smart, pleasant, decorated meeting place – but somehow it had a sterile, unwelcoming feel.

Most of Davies' team were already waiting for the first briefing of the day, chatting about how they were looking forward to some time away from the station when they were actually allowed a day off or last night's football which had produced the usual crop of unexpected results.

In the room there were fans of all the East Midlands teams, Nottingham Forest, Leicester City, Derby County, Mansfield Town and Notts County as well as those who supported Manchester United and Liverpool from afar. The usual banter about the teams' strengths and weaknesses helped to lighten the atmosphere.

Brooksby appreciated how hard the detectives and support staff were working. He was eager to compliment them on their endeavours, knowing that with two big investigations to solve they'd have plenty of tiring days and nights in front of them.

Miles called for quiet. 'Okay, let's bring you all up to speed on where we are. First, Felicity Strutt. James, what's the latest?'

'Billy Phillips: arrested this morning. No bother – came quietly. Thankfully we managed to keep the national press away. They didn't have a clue what was going on.

'CSIs are going through his house. Obviously it may be a few days before we get anything back. But there were no funny smells, so it's not immediately apparent if he's hidden any of Felicity's body parts there. We'll interview him later.'

'Thanks, James. As you know, Phillips is our number one suspect – but not the only one. Anything on her husband?'

Miles looked around. Catherine Thomas, a PC who interviewed Rob Woodcock when Felicity first went missing, answered.

'I went to see him again. I'm no expert but he looks a broken man. Went back to work after Felicity's disappearance but, according to his boss, his mind is hardly ever on the job. He even hired a private detective to try to find Felicity.'

'And what was the outcome of that?'

'The private eye dug around, found evidence that she'd met up with her boss at a hotel on Mansfield Road and told Woodcock she'd probably been having an affair.

'He refused to believe it. Said if it *was* true, it was just a phase she was going through. He was confident of getting her back and said he'd forgive her.

'Still no activity on her mobile phone or bank account.'

Miles looked at a folder in front of him, found the name of Felicity's boss at the TV station and continued: 'Thanks Catherine. What about Chris Watson – how's he taken Felicity's disappearance?'

'Couldn't cope at all. Some people might think that he'd got everything going for him, former professional rugby player running a TV station, seemingly had a great life. He's been diagnosed with depression.'

Miles wondered what it was about Felicity that meant she had such a captivating effect on those two men.

Catherine Thomas continued: 'Boss, I know you spoke to the staff at the TV station when she went missing and few people had a good word for her. I've been talking to them again: it seems Felicity never socialised with anyone she worked with. She was totally driven, determined to make it big as a presenter. That was all she was focused on – apart from doing a bit of charity work. But that usually meant her picture would be in the paper and across social media. She was certainly one for raising her own profile.'

'Thanks, Catherine. It seems as though we can probably rule out both Woodcock and Watson.'

He composed himself before continuing. 'Next: Daisy Higgins. Found over at Hilton. Murdered, then her body was thrown in a brook. Minus her fingers. On the face of it, it's a different *MO* to Felicity's death but we can't ignore the fact that Billy Phillips might be involved.

'We've got a good start on this because both Tilly and I knew Daisy from the Derby Storm basketball club where she worked.'

'What can you tell us about Daisy?' a voice from the back of the room asked.

Miles put his file on the desk. No need now to refer to his notes.

'Mid thirties. Doting mother to a seven-year-old boy Joey. Very good relationship with her mother who often took care of her grandson if Daisy was working late.

'Good worker. Everyone at the Storm spoke highly of her. No idea where Joey's dad is – he hasn't been on the scene for years. As far as I'm aware, she wasn't involved with anyone else.

'We'd already got her car in the garage – it broke down as she was driving home. She'd only just had it serviced but the mechanic who did the job didn't tighten up the sump plug properly and all the oil spilled out.

'I've ordered a full forensic inspection of the car. Interesting to see if anyone else's fingerprints or DNA are on it.

'The main point we need to establish is whether anyone was following her before she broke down or if it was an opportunist who saw her at the side of the road and attacked her.

'Tilly's making further inquiries into Daisy's background and we'll both be going to the Storm's game against Birmingham Bullets tomorrow. If anyone wants to join us . . .'

Some of the team quickly made their excuses: 'You won't catch me watching oversized freaks playing a daft American sport.' 'I've arranged to see the mother-in-law.' 'Oh, I'm staying in to wash my hair,' said a male detective who was almost bald.

23

Although the headquarters of the East Midlands Constabulary was on the outskirts of Nottingham, the powers-that-be decided the force also needed a city-centre presence. That was why a multi-million pound custody centre was given the go-ahead on a piece of land owned by the city council that was originally earmarked for luxury office accommodation.

It had no fewer than a hundred cells – ample to cater for any miscreants on a boozy weekend or football hooligans visiting the city in the guise of 'supporting' their team.

There were cells for both men and women prisoners and there was a separate entrance for vulnerable adults. Each cell had CCTV and an intercom which could be used to contact detention officers. Some of those arrested thought they were staying in a hotel and made excessive demands for food and drinks.

Staff treated everyone the same no matter how serious the alleged offence they were facing. If anyone said politely 'can I have a lasagne?' and it wasn't on the menu, detention officers would serve up something similar. It was only when cheeky inmates asked for lobster thermidor that they were told the nearest thing they could manage was a tuna sandwich.

Resident doctors and nurses were always on hand along with drug and alcohol experts whose primary function was to support offenders with dependency problems. Despite that, many of the custody suite visitors were regulars who'd turned to petty crime to fund their habit.

One outraged politician described it as a 'five-star hotel for criminals' and a 'waste of taxpayers' hard-earned cash'. But the building had the backing of the Police and Crime Commissioner who said it was fit for purpose and staff would want to work in its welcoming environment.

There were also offices which could be commandeered as incident rooms for ongoing investigations, meaning detectives didn't have to traipse all the way over from HQ whenever they needed to interview a suspect.

Psychologists had identified the colours that they said would ensure those who'd been arrested would remain calm: orange, teal and green. Sections of the custody suite had been decorated in those colours – but hardened detention officers reckoned that anyone arrested after a Saturday night pub brawl wouldn't even register what shade the corridor was where they'd been incarcerated.

The duty custody sergeant, an experienced officer who'd been asked to take on the role on a temporary basis but had remained in it for several years, briefed his team who were beginning their day shift.

'We've got three who were brought in for assault after knocking seven bells out of each other. One of those bars in the city centre where I wouldn't trust the bouncers to keep my grandmother quiet. They're in cells eleven, twenty-four and thirty-six. We need to make sure they're kept apart – we don't want them kicking off again, although hopefully they'll have slept off the effects of the skinful they had last night.'

He listed everyone else who'd been detained overnight, including a giant of a man who'd allegedly hit his partner in a domestic incident, three drink-drivers, a couple of teenagers suspected of supplying cocaine and a woman who was a regular visitor to the suite who'd stolen a bottle of gin from an all-night convenience store.

Billy Phillips was booked in and stood to attention while the necessary formalities were carried out. The desk sergeant noted that Phillips seemed detached, unsure about what was going on and had to be asked on a couple of occasions to confirm his name, date of birth and address.

'Have you ever tried to harm yourself?'

Phillips mumbled that he hadn't.

'Do you have any mental health issues that I need to be made aware of?'

Phillips muttered something about schizophrenia which the custody sergeant struggled to make out.

'Any issues with alcohol or drugs?'

Philips shook his head.

'Have you got a solicitor?'

'What?'

'A solicitor. Have you got one?'

'No. Do I need one?'

'You're facing a very serious charge. If you've not got your own legal representation, we'll get the duty solicitor to come. I think we'll also get the nurse to have a look at you.'

He summoned the nurse from her office, told her about Phillips' answers to his questions and suggested the mental health team might want to assess Phillips to see whether he was fit for detention and interview.

Phillips said nothing and continued to stare straight ahead.

24

It was the job that Miles hated above everything else. He could just about stomach seeing in a mortuary the bodies of people who'd been killed in horrendous circumstances. He was okay with attending post-mortem examinations where the smell of death was unmistakeable. But telling a relative that a loved one had died came top of his list of tasks to avoid.

Everyone in the force thought the same way: how do you make 'I'm sorry for your loss' sound sincere?

He thought about a funeral director he knew whose son was destined to take over the business when he retired. One day he said to Miles: 'I'm worried about our Jeremy. If you ask him to dress a body and prepare it for a funeral, he's brilliant. Makes a wonderful job of it. But if he has to speak to a family who've been bereaved – which is an essential part of the job – he'll do anything to get out of it.' I know where he's coming from, Miles thought.

Tilly noticed Miles' downtrodden look, his eyes full of sadness and resignation.

'What's the matter, boss?'

When he told her, she gave the answer he was hoping for: 'Do you want me to come with you, give you a bit of moral support?'

Christine Higgins lived in a recently built, two-bedroomed bungalow just a couple of miles from Daisy. It had a well-maintained lawn and pretty flower beds, roses, fuchsias and dahlias which would continue to look eye-catching until the first frost of winter arrived.

It should have been Christine and her husband Brian's retirement present to themselves, somewhere they could grow old gracefully and welcome both Daisy and Joey whenever they wanted to visit.

But that was before Brian unexpectedly suffered a fatal heart attack. The former university sociology professor had ensured that Christine was looked after financially – but she was devastated when he passed away.

She'd taken on board the old saying that you shouldn't make major decisions after the death of a loved one for at least a year, possibly two. Now she was weighing up whether the bungalow had too many painful memories for her to continue living there.

Miles stopped the car outside, turned off the engine and unclipped his seat belt. He hesitated before opening the door, then felt Tilly put her hand on his arm. They walked side by side up the path to the bungalow.

Christine greeted them almost as soon as they pressed the doorbell. Her eyes were red, with dark bags underneath them. She told Joey to go and play while she showed the detectives into the lounge.

'There's no easy way of telling you this,' Miles said, his voice catching in his throat as he tried to break the news as quicky and sensitively as possible.

He explained that a body had been found and it was almost certainly Daisy's. Christine tried to catch her breath and after a couple of seconds began wailing like a young child who'd had a painful fall. Her sobs could probably be heard halfway down the street as she fell into Miles' arms.

He thought to himself that this really wasn't the time to tell her he needed a DNA sample from both Christine and Joey.

'I'll put the kettle on,' Tilly said.

25

Miles and Tilly sprinted across the Derby Storm car park. The rain clouds that had been threatening all day to split open and soak anyone beneath them were unable to hold off any longer.

As they went into the modern, spacious, pristine entrance, Miles noticed that the Cloud Centre was as busy as usual. It'll take more than the heaviest rainstorm you could imagine to put these supporters off their basketball, Miles thought.

It was the Storm's second home game in three days. The talk around the Fast Break coffee shop and on the bleachers before a game was usually how the team were doing, whether the American players were pulling their weight and if the Storm would be able to secure home advantage in the play-offs.

But as Derby prepared for the game against a re-formed Birmingham Bullets, many fans remarked that Daisy Higgins wasn't there. No one could remember the last fixture she'd missed; she was always in place to welcome supporters into the building. It was a crisis that Daisy hadn't shown up.

Miles and Tilly heard rumours that she'd been fired because she'd stolen money from the club; the owner had been having an affair with her and paid her off when she said she was going to tell his wife; and some of the club's long-serving staff had threatened to leave because she wielded so much power.

All totally fabricated, the two detectives knew. They'd yet to reveal the news that she'd been found dead.

They took every opportunity to talk to diehard fans they were acquainted with or to listen to any gossip which might shed some light on Daisy's lifestyle.

During the half-time break Miles and Tilly went to different parts of the Cloud Centre. Tilly could hardly wait to tell Miles what she'd heard.

'You know Emily, don't you? Goes to all the games, especially the away ones. She reckons she saw Daisy out with Cameron White last night. She reckons they didn't want anyone to see them together.'

Cameron White was the Storm's star player. A six foot five inch guard, he'd been a huge success since he arrived in the country at the start of the season. He was considered not quite good enough for the NBA in the States and rather than go to Greece or France where he didn't know the language, he decided to come to England for a year or two and have some fun before deciding what he wanted to do with the rest of his life. He could also check out whether he had any English ancestors, a belief held by his grandparents.

With his boyish looks, excellent physique and exciting style, he was everyone's favourite player. Some Storm fans even compared him to Ernest Lee, a Derby legend who was recognised as being one of the best players ever to come to England.

Lee had taken his own life after failing to convince NBA scouts he was good enough for their roster. Those who idolised him in 1989 and 1990 were of the opinion that he was perhaps born too early; there were more opportunities to shine now, especially in the G-League which comprised teams affiliated to NBA franchises.

Miles had also heard supporters chatting during the break. They were unanimous in their view that White was playing well below his potential and wasn't dominating the game the way he usually did.

One of the team who drew up statistics for each game produced the story of the first half for Miles. White had scored only eight points – his average for a forty-minute game was twenty-nine – and he'd dished off only one assist. And that was to a team mate who hammered home an uncontested slam dunk at the end of a fast break.

Could something be playing on White's mind? Miles knew that Birmingham had a reasonable team but they didn't have anyone strong enough defensively to shackle White. Maybe he was tired.

Playing two games in three days wasn't an unusual occurrence for a basketball team. They didn't moan like footballers about having to play fixtures in quick succession. But maybe the exertion of running the team on the court was proving too much for White. Perhaps he wasn't the superstar everyone thought he was.

Miles admonished himself for the way he tended to give basketball players the benefit of the doubt. Why couldn't he look at them in the same way that he viewed anyone else who might be a suspect when a crime had been committed? Especially the murder of a friend. If White was the last person to see Daisy alive, he'd be a significant part of the murder investigation.

The referee's whistle called the two teams back to the court for the second half. Miles and Tilly agreed they needed to speak to the American after the game.

Whatever the Storm's coach said to his players in the locker room at half time had an immediate impact. Trailing by twelve points, Derby hit back, with White orchestrating the offence. He hit two huge three-pointers and got the ball inside on two occasions to the Storm's centre who powered his way to the basket. White then stole the ball from the Bullets' point guard and raced through for a tomahawk dunk which had the whole crowd on their feet.

Derby wiped out the deficit in the first four minutes of the third quarter and didn't relinquish the lead. The coach substituted White with five minutes to go, the Storm being in an unassailable position.

Miles and Tilly marvelled at White's on-court dexterity. But how would he react when told about Daisy's death?

They didn't have to wait long after the end of the game for White to appear from the locker room. The Storm's owner had allowed the detectives to use his office; they were grateful to talk to White away from prying eyes and inquisitive ears.

Wearing a teal polo shirt featuring the Storm's logo, dark jeans and new, spotless trainers, White looked the consummate athlete. But he was unable to hide a look of trepidation, even a slight hint of fear, as Miles and Tilly introduced themselves.

'Good second half,' Miles began. 'Birmingham just didn't know how to handle you.'

'Thanks,' White replied, unsure at that stage whether the detectives knew anything about basketball or whether they were making small talk.

'But what was going on in the first half?' Tilly shot back. 'Couple of air balls, you turned the ball over too many times, didn't rebound – it seemed as though your mind was elsewhere.'

White took his time before answering, appearing to consider just how much he should tell the police. Miles noticed that White's voice remained calm throughout although his drawn-out drawl made him sound as though he was speaking very slowly.

'I admit that my mind was elsewhere. Before the game we'd all heard about Daisy's disappearance and I allowed it to affect my performance. Coach had a go at me at the break. Told me I shouldn't take personal problems onto the court. He was right, of course.'

'And did that news affect you more than your team mates?' asked Miles, focusing on White's deep-blue eyes which still showed an element of tension.

'She's one of the Storm family. We've all been upset by her disappearance.'

'But maybe not as much as you. Any truth in the rumour that you and Daisy were an item?' Tilly asked.

'Who told you that?'

'Never mind who. Is it true?'

'Well, we have been out together a few times. We're very fond of each other – I wouldn't go any further than that.'

Miles suddenly lost his reluctance to grill basketball players and led the questioning.

'And how did Daisy feel about the relationship?'

'The same as me. We just wanted to hang out together, have a bit of fun.'

'Are you sure about that? You don't think Daisy wanted to take the relationship more seriously but things started to move too quickly for you?'

'Not at all. We hadn't made any plans, especially as I don't know what I'll be doing in 12 months' time. I may be back in Derby. I could be in a different country altogether.'

'So what were your movements after the game two nights ago?'

'Daisy and I had a quick drink in the bar, then she said she had to go. Her mother was looking after Joey and Daisy didn't want her mom getting home too late.'

Miles stared at White for a moment, giving the American time to think he was off the hook.

'I'm sorry to tell you that Daisy's been murdered.'

The colour drained from the player's face. His eyes were racked with pain and disbelief as he screwed up his face in sorrow.

Miles continued: 'I'm sure you won't object if we ask for a DNA sample and take your fingerprints. What would you say if I told you that you were the last person to see Daisy before she vanished?'

The American took a few seconds to compose himself: 'Impossible. Someone else must have seen her. When she left here she was fine. In fact her last words were: "I'm going to a meeting tomorrow night. I'll see you at the Birmingham game".'

26

The following morning Miles was in his office early when his phone rang. He snatched the handset off its cradle, anxious to get rid of the caller so that he could check whether any information had come in overnight on the two cases his team were working on.

It was a call he wasn't expecting – and one which sent a shudder through his whole body. He was summoned to the Chief Constable's office – immediately.

Pausing only to inform James West that the start of the briefing might have to be delayed, he made his way to the lift that would take him to the top floor of police HQ.

What did the big boss want now, he wondered. It was a Saturday; it must be something major for the Chief to call in Miles at a weekend.

In his mind Miles went through the current investigations, the torso in the suitcase and the murder of Daisy Higgins. He'd done everything by the book; he didn't think he or any of his fiercely loyal team had put a foot wrong in either case.

He was even looking at the two cases in tandem. He could think of many forces that would assign two separate senior officers to the cases and bring them together only if it were established that they were linked. He was content to carry on looking at the two crimes even though he felt sure they were committed by two different people.

Felicity Strutt, hacked to death by a monster who had no respect for her life. Daisy Higgins, murdered possibly by an opportunistic killer who removed her fingers. But the rest of her was intact. It was likely that whoever took her life was aware forensically of what needed to be done to avoid capture.

The lift jolted as it stopped on the top floor, home to the Chief, his assistant and deputy chief constables, the Police and Crime Commissioner, her chief executive, chief finance officer, head of commissioning and support staff.

When the building was erected to house the East Midlands Constabulary – an amalgamation of the Nottinghamshire, Leicestershire and Derbyshire forces – it was stressed that the upper echelons of the organisation should be on the top floors. Miles couldn't understand why. From his limited experience of business protocol he always felt it was better for the allegedly more important members of a company to be visible, to interact with the general workforce as much as possible. But he was just a copper, so what did he know?

He had a depressing feeling of *déjà vu* as he was shown into the Chief's office. Again he offered Miles a seat which he reluctantly accepted while his superior remained standing.

'What's all this?' he barked as he threw the day's edition of the East Midlands Express onto his desk.

Miles hadn't had the chance to look at the paper that morning as he was so engrossed in the two investigations.

He recoiled in horror as he saw the headline and hoped the Chief hadn't spotted his reaction.

Crime boss: 'traumatised' worker to sue police

Miles quickly read through the story. Under the headline, in a prominent position that no one could miss, was the revelation that it was written by 'our chief reporter Tony Goodson'.

The article outlined how Monica Evans who was a 'domestic worker' for Ken Thompson, a crime boss who'd terrorised many areas of the East Midlands, suffered post-traumatic stress disorder when police shot Thompson dead.

He'd taken her hostage and was aiming to evade arrest – until a basketball thrown by Miles caught him off guard, allowing a police firearms unit to 'take him out'.

Mrs Evans was taking a civil action against the police allegedly for 'excessive use of force'.

The Chief, stern, sullen and surly, waited until Miles lifted up his eyes from the page.

'Well?'

Miles couldn't think of what to say. There were few times when he'd been left speechless; this was one of them.

'Well, what, sir?' he said and instantly regretted opening his mouth.

'We're getting so much flak lately from people who reckon they're not satisfied with our performance. And now this. It's the last thing we need.'

Miles had thought about interrupting but was glad he'd waited until the Chief had finished.

'Sir, all I can say is: the IOPC cleared us of any wrongdoing. As a force, we were exonerated. We can't be responsible for everyone who has a grudge against us and persuades a gullible journalist to write a front-page splash slagging us off.'

'I'll have something to say to the media relations team about the story. In the meantime we need to build bridges with certain sections of the community. It's time we got some good news in the press. And I think you're the man to do it.'

Miles groaned to himself, fearing what was to come.

'The number of complaints we're getting from younger members of society is increasing. Particularly from those who've been caught up in a stop and search. I want you to reach out to them, remove the stigma around the police. Engage with them, show them we're human beings. You never know, some of them may ultimately decide they want a career in the police.

'Now, any ideas?'

Miles looked blank.

'Have a think about it. Work out a plan. It won't take you long. I'm sure it'll be a success.'

No pressure, then, Miles thought.

'Now, I think you've got a briefing to attend.'

'Thank you, sir.' Miles was thankful to leave the Chief's domain. He was glad he'd kept quiet about how busy his team were. It wouldn't have been wise to object to having yet another task to sort out. And he knew exactly what would appeal to the city's youngsters.

27

Miles grabbed his bag with his crime-scene essentials and a cup of tea he'd hastily made in a thermal mug. He got into his eight-year-old Ford Focus – advised by a friend who was a mechanic to get one of those cars because they needed little maintenance – and pressed the start button.

He heard the *do-be-do, do-be-do* reminding him that the Focus needed an oil change. But the car started first time.

As he drove towards Hilton he tried to imagine what sort of person would want to kill Daisy. A previous partner? He discounted that theory because, as far as he knew, Daisy hadn't been in a relationship for a long time. Unless you included Cameron White. It was possible that the Storm player wanted a more serious relationship than Daisy did. But Miles knew she was a strong, single-minded person and she would have let White know exactly where he stood.

Could it have been someone who followed her home from the Storm? Unlikely. Miles' team would know more when they'd checked automatic number plate recognition cameras and CCTV to see whether they could shed any light on what happened.

His thoughts kept returning to Daisy's car breaking down. Was it bad luck that her killer was just passing by and decided to take out his anger, frustration or sadistic tendencies on Daisy? And who would have chopped off her fingers? Someone with a good knowledge of forensics? A doctor who'd been struck off? A vet? Someone who was or who had been in the police?

The only conclusion Miles came to was that Daisy was in the wrong place at the wrong time.

His journey took him along the A50 and past the Toyota factory. He was only a lad when the Japanese car giant decided to build its first European factory at Burnaston in 1989. Now it employed thousands of people and contributed more than five billion pounds to the Derbyshire economy.

Miles knew he had to do whatever he could to remove the cordon around Hilton so that the village could get back to something approaching normality.

The crime scene manager, a man in his forties with slicked-back hair and a bulbous nose, met Miles on a street called The Mease and brought him up to date.

'CSIs have done a good job. They've established that Daisy wasn't killed here – she was thrown into the brook about two hundred metres away and the current brought her body here.

'The Home Office pathologist reckons she was probably strangled in the old part of the village. There were marks by the side of the brook indicating that there'd been a struggle. But the rain's washed away any footprints. We've just found a few spots of blood. They've gone off to the lab to see whether they were Daisy's.'

Miles gave a slight smile. 'Thanks. Good work. Keep the cordon around the old part of the village for now. We'll open up the rest. I'm sure a lot of people will be pleased to hear that.'

He called the station and spoke to Tilly.

'Get someone to check whether there've been other incidents of murder victims having their fingers removed. There's a chance we might have a serial killer to worry about. I don't recall anything – but it could be that, for whatever reason, the murderer may have stopped for a while and now he's up to his old tricks again.'

'How far do you want me to go back?'

'Start with the last five years. If you don't find anything, go further back – ten, twenty, even twenty-five years. It could be that this guy was convicted of a serious offence, has served his time and has taken up where he left off.'

Whenever a suspect was arrested, there was still plenty of work to do to find witnesses and build up a picture of the person who was in custody. Miles asked Mark Roberts to look into Billy Phillips' background knowing that Roberts would approach it methodically, with a meticulous attitude and mindful of the responsibility he'd been given.

Roberts was relishing the assignment, all the more so because he was working alone and not with Paul Allen who'd sometimes go off at a tangent simply so that he could make a witty remark or tell a funny story.

It also meant that Roberts could get out of the office and go to meet some of Phillips' neighbours.

Both Brooksby and Miles insisted their team should dress smartly. With a conservative sports jacket, dark trousers, light blue shirt and plain tie, Roberts could have passed himself off as a council officer or water board official rather than a detective. His low, non-confrontational voice meant that sometimes people trusted him and opened up to him.

What he gleaned was that most residents thought Phillips was wacky, eccentric or even insane.

Roberts discovered that Phillips had been living with his mother until she died about eighteen months previously. She'd suffered from breast cancer and he'd been her carer although if anyone saw him in a shop he was always complaining about her ruining his life and he never had time to pursue his own interests. Yet no one got to find out what those interests were.

His mother had a very old car but had stopped driving several years earlier. People had seen Phillips at the wheel taking his mum to hospital appointments, but it appeared he wasn't a confident driver and preferred to use the bus.

Police had impounded the car which was being examined forensically. Roberts had few doubts that Felicity Strutt's DNA would be all over it.

As he passed Phillips' house, Roberts noticed members of the CSI team in their white suits bringing out black bags full of stuff to be analysed as part of the investigation.

He was about to chat to one of the CSIs when a woman in her sixties with lank hair, an anorak which gave little protection from the elements and jogging bottoms came up to him.

'You with the police?'

Roberts knew the suit and tie gave him away. Very few people dressed like that in this part of the city – not even for weddings or funerals. He introduced himself and showed her his warrant card.

'That bloke living there, a real odd character.'

'In what way?'

'He was a mummy's boy all his life. When she died, seemed as though he couldn't cope.

'Never had a girlfriend and never likely to. What he needed was a good woman to sort him out. But his mum never encouraged him to go out with girls. Although he might have wanted female company, he didn't have the confidence to talk to women.'

Roberts jumped in while she took a breath.

'What about men – do you think he might have been gay?'

'Nah. My son's gay. Nothing like this bloke. I noticed a few months ago that his behaviour was getting stranger. Always kept the curtains closed, especially the ones upstairs.

'You're too young to remember this but when I was a girl and there was a death in the family, you kept your curtains closed until after the funeral. It was a mark of respect, signified that you were in mourning.

'That bloke didn't open his curtains and I thought it was because his mother had died. But it went on for months.

138

'I started to believe there was something really funny going on in that house.'

28

'Okay, listen up.'

Miles brought the room to order for the evening briefing. 'James, what's the latest on Felicity Strutt?'

'Boss, the CSIs have gone through Billy Phillips' home with a fine-toothed comb. A head, arms and legs were found in a freezer. Not much doubt that they'll be Felicity's. Presumably Phillips was going to get rid of them after he'd disposed of the torso. They're with the pathologist now.

'We're taking a look at a car parked on the street near his home. His mother is the registered keeper. He didn't bother to change it into his own name after she died. He hasn't even got a licence.

'As far as we can make out, Phillips abducted Felicity after she left the hotel on Mansfield Road, took her back to his place and at some stage killed her and cut her into pieces. We've recovered a knife and a meat cleaver.

'Now he's in custody, we're hoping he'll tell us why he did it.'

The room had gone quiet as West revealed the gory details.

'Thanks, James. I'd like you and Mark to interview him. We've got enough to charge him but we need to go that bit further, find out what his motive was for killing Felicity.

"I've been talking to a friend of mine who's a psychologist. She reckons it's a big leap from killing someone to chopping up their body. So we need to know what was the trigger that made him do it.

'You can also ask him what his movements were on the night Daisy Higgins was murdered. He probably won't have an alibi but I don't think we'll be able to get any evidence that he was in Hilton.'

He turned to another page of notes in his file: 'The results of the post-mortem on Daisy have revealed there was no water in her lungs – she was strangled before she went into the water. She was wearing a Storm scarf. The killer used that.

'I don't need to remind you that strangulation is a deliberate act. Unlike some other forms of taking a person's life, it can't be done accidentally. The killer has to make a decision when they're with the victim: that decision is to walk away or continue. If they carry on, they're witnessing the exact moment when the victim is unable to fight back, when that person takes their last breath before becoming still.

'Her clothes are being examined. Let's hope the killer's DNA is on them.'

He gulped before continuing: 'She was also sexually assaulted. So she went through a terrifying ordeal before she died.

'And we need to locate her fingers. Did the killer throw them away or has he – or she – taken them home?'

'Are we doing a fingertip search?'

Paul Allen's quip hung in the air. His colleagues were silent, aghast that he'd actually made such a callous remark.

'Any more comments like that, Paul, and you're off the team.'

A voice chimed in from the back of the room: 'Boss, any idea as to the killer's motive?'

There was a touch of venom in Miles' voice as he replied. 'Not that we've come across yet. So what happened – did the killer panic? Did they think they'd be found out? Did they do away with her to get rid of the evidence? It would seem that way because they tried to destroy DNA by throwing her into the river.

'From what I know of Daisy, she didn't have a bad bone in her body. I'm sure she wouldn't have antagonised her killer in any way.

'What about you, Mark – any theories?'

142

Mark Roberts weighed everything up before speaking. 'If she was as good a person as you reckon – and I've got no reason to doubt that – could it be a case of mistaken identity?'

'Possibly,' said Miles. 'We can't rule it out at this stage.'

Another member of the team voiced her thoughts: 'Do we have to consider that she might have been killed to order, that someone might have wanted her out of the way?'

'Good point, although you'd think a hitman would be more inclined to use a gun. A professional hitman, anyway. Someone who didn't have a lot of experience who was touting themselves around as a killer might have chosen strangulation – but would he then cut her fingers off? I doubt it.

'I reckon it's a control thing: the killer wants the victim to know who's in control, who has the power of life or death. We've got to find out if this person was determined to murder someone and Daisy unfortunately satisfied his or her lust to kill.'

29

Detective Superintendent Brooksby gave the go-ahead for a news conference to see whether a public appeal would turn up any new leads in the hunt for Daisy Higgins' killer.

Officers had trawled through hundreds of hours of CCTV footage and taken scores of statements without coming up with any suspects. Both Brooksby and Miles realised that after the press conference they would get all sorts of weird calls from people with nothing better to do than waste the police's time – but they were getting desperate for a breakthrough.

Miles had persuaded Christine to speak to the press about Daisy – she'd agreed only if Miles would be sitting alongside her. He'd sorted out with the media relations team a strategy for the morning's event which was timed to meet the deadline for the regional television stations' lunchtime news: talk about how senseless the murder was; explain how Daisy, a caring and respected mother, daughter and colleague, had everything to live for; and appeal to anyone with information to come forward.

Then Miles would introduce Christine who would talk about the loss of her wonderful, irreplaceable daughter. He knew that the more emotional Christine became, the more the television cameras would like it. He would stress how eager the police were to catch whoever was responsible for this horrendous crime. He would conclude by reiterating the appeal for witnesses.

The room reserved for press conferences was on one of the upper floors of the East Midlands Police headquarters. It was deliberately sited well out of the way – managers were determined that no inquisitive journalists would be able to pick up snippets of information by overhearing operational matters being discussed.

Few staff found it necessary to visit this particular floor. It housed the Chief Officer Team meeting room. Alongside it, securely locked most of the time, was the room where the press had to have a special invitation to attend.

A BBC camera operator, looking tired and bedraggled, hauled his equipment out of the lift. He was grateful it was working – he struggled to carry his camera and tripod up only one flight of stairs – and that there wasn't a long corridor to negotiate. Like most of his colleagues, he suffered from back strain after years of carrying his gear to inaccessible buildings, along uneven country paths and odd locations far away from where he had to leave his estate car.

In one way he envied some of the broadcast journalists who used more modern, smaller cameras as they

145

filmed their own stories. But to compensate for that, their pictures were always inferior quality. Whenever he watched a television documentary he could instantly tell whether the shot on screen had been captured with a high-quality camera, a smaller version or on a mobile phone.

Seven other people were waiting for the press conference to start: a reporter and camera operator from ITV News; a video journalist from a regional community television station; reporters from BBC local radio and the commercial station which served the East Midlands; a reporter from BBC online because the Corporation considered it such a big story that the news editor wanted it to go 'live' as quickly as possible; and Tony Goodson from the East Midlands Express.

Miles explained that he'd outline the facts of the case, then he'd introduce Christine and afterwards he'd answer questions before giving one-to-one interviews to any of the journalists who wanted them. But Christine wouldn't be speaking after the press conference.

He told reporters what was known about Daisy's last movements, how the police had yet to discover any reason why someone would want to harm her and then asked for the public's help.

Christine, with tears in her eyes even before Miles started speaking, declared that she couldn't have wished for a more considerate daughter and she didn't know how Daisy's bright, loving son would learn to cope without his mother. She appealed for anyone with information, however trivial it might seem, to come forward and tell the police.

She stopped a couple of times to wipe her eyes and blow her nose. Miles imagined her face would be everywhere as the story made headline news.

When it was time for questions, a couple of journalists asked for clarifications which Miles dealt with as quickly as he could.

Then: 'Tony Goodson, chief reporter, East Midlands Express.' The pride in his 'chief reporter' title wasn't lost on anyone in the room.

'Detective Inspector Davies, are you really telling us everything you know about this case?'

Miles was taken aback but hoped his expression remained deadpan.

'In every case there are certain details which can't be released because it might harm the investigation. This is no different to any other.'

'Come, Inspector. Usually in an investigation such as this you hold something back, maybe something specific that only the killer would know. But don't you think the public have a right to know if there's a serial killer on the loose?

'I and my fellow journalists cover murder stories all the time. This one's obviously not a domestic. What makes it any different? Shouldn't you be revealing all the gory details? That might encourage more people to come forward and tell you what they know.'

Miles noticed Christine was close to breaking point.

He'd seen Goodson's name on front-page exclusives but this was the first time he'd come across Goodson in person. Miles' first impression of the reporter wasn't a favourable one. How did he know this wasn't a domestic? For all Goodson knew, Daisy might have had a suspicious partner who followed her and killed her for any number of reasons.

'Mr Goodson, there's absolutely no evidence to suggest that we could be dealing with a serial killer. We're treating this as an isolated event and the public shouldn't be concerned for their safety.

'We've told you as much as we possibly can. Police work can be tedious. I'm sure you wouldn't want to alienate your readers in any way, so there's no point telling you the ages, gender and occupation of everyone we've taken statements from who were in the area without seeing anything.

'I'm not trying to tell you how to do your job. I'm simply saying that readers of your esteemed publication wouldn't want to be bombarded with all the boring details of this case.

'Now, unless there are any other questions, I'll be available for individual interviews next door.'

30

'Tilly, what have we got on killers who cut off their victims' fingers?'

'Not a lot, boss. Seems it's something that doesn't happen very often. There were two cases, both in 2003, of brutal attacks involving amputations. A British saxophonist was in Australia when armed men set on him and chopped off three of his fingers but he survived. In San Diego a guy was sentenced to death for killing his girlfriend and removing her fingers. They were found in a rubbish bin.

'The only thing I've found in this country was in 2020. A guy in Newcastle snipped off the fingers and toes of his victims – but the killer wasn't leaving a message. The judge described it as a "sustained and particularly horrific attack". He jailed the killer for life and told him he'd serve at least twenty-six years in prison.

'In Ireland two butchers chopped off the fingertips and thumbs of a seventeen-year-old lad. The prosecution said they'd done it to remove any of their DNA from under their fingernails so that they could avoid capture.'

She was now in full flow: 'There was an interesting case in Portugal. A young woman strangled her former lover, then got rid of the body with the help of the new man in her life. They chopped off his fingers and then used them to access his bank account using an app on his mobile phone. They knew what they were doing: the hotel worker's father had died and left him money in his will – sixty grand.'

Someone whistled. Other detectives gasped in surprise.

Miles jumped in: 'Doesn't sound like a copycat killing, then. Could be that Daisy tried to defend herself and the killer removed her fingers to get rid of evidence.

'As for the other theory, we know there was no activity on Daisy's bank account shortly after she died but let's have another look. We need a complete check on Daisy's finances. That could give us a motive: the killer might have known she'd got money and could have used her fingers to get at it.'

Helen Loudon searched through her wardrobe to find something suitable to wear. She came across tops and skirts she hadn't worn for what appeared to be several years although since Jack's death time had little meaning for her.

It's only a catch-up with Monica Evans, she told herself, so there was no reason to dress to impress. But she still had the urge to feel and look good even though their intention was merely to visit a couple of pubs in the city centre.

She also expected Monica not to go to any trouble with her appearance. It was strange, she thought, how they'd become good friends despite appearing to have little in common.

They arranged to do what so many people in Nottingham had done over the decades: meet at the left lion. Two stone lions either side of the steps leading to the front entrance of the Council House in the Old Market Square had been a fixture for as long as anyone could remember.

They were the handiwork of Nottingham sculptor Joseph Else who was principal of the city's School of Art from 1923 to 1939.

Each weighing two tonnes, the lions were large enough for adults as well as children to clamber over. They were also a convenient meeting place, especially in the days before mobile phones. Many couples met there at the start of their first date, their affection for the lions not diminishing as their relationships progressed into marriage.

The left lion was known as Leo or Lennie, the right one Oscar or Ronnie. Officially they were named after two brothers who in Greek mythology were kings, Agamemnon and Menelaus.

Despite rain which had been falling heavily for the past hour, the Old Market Square was bustling when Helen and Monica noticed each other. They chatted about other people they'd met in the same place and Helen remarked that she'd never heard a peep out of either of the lions. Legend had it that the left one roared when a virgin went past and the right one made a similar noise when an honest politician walked by.

They laughed as they scurried to the Joseph Else, a Wetherspoon pub named in honour of the sculptor.

Helen insisted on buying the drinks, deciding on a gin and tonic while Monica opted for a pint of lager. They talked about how depressing the weather was, what they'd been up to earlier in the day and how relationships with members of their family could be so difficult.

'You can choose your friends but you can't choose your family,' Helen observed.

'Dead right,' Monica replied. 'Same wiv husbands. Pity a marriage licence doesn't 'ave to be renewed after a few years. Make divorce a bloody lot easier. And cheaper!'

They giggled like two schoolgirls who'd seen their teacher trip up in the playground only to act as though nothing had happened.

'So, presumably your marriage didn't last?' Helen probed.

'Nah. He was a right waste of time. Always down the pub. Leaving me to look after the kids, do the 'ousework and have his dinner on the table just when he wanted it.

'I'd 'ad enough and kicked 'im out. 'Ave as little as possible to do with 'im now. 'E used to see the boys sometimes but now they're older they can make up their own minds wevver they want to 'ave anything to do wiv 'im.

'It was a struggle bringin' up the boys but it was worf it to get rid of 'im. What about you?'

Helen fetched more drinks before answering. She told Monica how Jack's father had taken badly the news that she was pregnant and had never had anything to do with their son. She'd never even been on a date since.

'But I'll let you into a secret. There's someone I'm quite fond of. And I think it could lead to something a bit more serious.'

'Good on yer. Who is it?'

Helen composed herself, trying to contain the excitement that built up inside her every time she thought about him.

'It's Tony. You know, the reporter. He's been so good to me. Considerate, caring. Makes me feel special. After what happened with Jack's dad, I've always been careful. Don't want to let myself in for another situation like that.

'Tony's different. I know he's proud of his work and likes having his stories on the front page, but his heart's in the right place. He's coming round for dinner soon. I'm really looking forward to it.'

'You be careful. 'E might come over as a decent bloke, but fink of what fings might be like after you've bin wiv 'im for a few years.

'You mark my words: men don't change. They can put on airs and graces and you don't know what they're really like until it's too late. Make sure you know what this Tony is really like under the surface.'

31

Miles looked around the room as his team filtered in for the evening briefing. He noticed energy levels were low but knew everyone would perk up when he told them the Crown Prosecution Service had authorised that Phillips should be charged with Felicity Strutt's murder. He also knew that the feeling of euphoria wouldn't last long and they'd soon flag off.

He was feeling exhausted himself but he knew he had to keep going. He'd never been more intent on solving a case; he wanted to put Daisy's killer behind bars more than any other criminal he'd come across in his career.

He also resolved to get enough evidence to convince a judge that whoever was responsible for her death would spend the maximum time possible in prison.

His mind drifted. He'd never been in favour of a life for a life and he couldn't comprehend how it had taken until 1965 for Parliament to abolish the death penalty for murder in England, Wales and Scotland. That was a couple of decades before he was born but he couldn't believe criminals were still being hanged during a period known for its hedonism and free love.

While Miles wasn't an advocate for a return to capital punishment, he was in favour of courts handing out the most serious punishments at their disposal.

Whole-life orders had been issued in about a hundred cases since they were introduced in 1983 and some prisoners had died in custody. Miles was resolute in wanting Daisy's killer to be added to that list. But would he or she have to kill again before a whole-life order could be issued?

'Okay. Tilly, bring us up to date with the investigation into Daisy Higgins' death.'

She jumped to her feet. 'No activity on her bank account, so we can assume robbery wasn't a motive and the killer didn't remove her fingers to steal money using an app on her phone. But her phone is still missing.

'We've got the forensic report into Daisy's car. Four lots of DNA in it: Daisy's, her son Joey's, her mum Christine's and her friend Cameron White's. But nothing else.'

Miles took a while before continuing. When he did, Tilly noticed a hint of desperation in his voice although she wasn't sure whether any of her colleagues heard it. 'We've now got to treat Cameron White as a person of interest. I want to know everything about him, what time he gets up, when he goes to bed, what car he drives, where he was on the night Daisy disappeared.

'And we need to find her phone. It could tell us so much about her final movements. It could also give us a motive. We still haven't got a clue why anyone would want to kill her.'

Tilly added: 'We've gone through her financial details again. Nothing's jumping out at us, so we're no further forward in finding a motive.

'We've picked Daisy up on CCTV going from the meeting in Sudbury but we still don't know what happened to her after that. We're checking the footage. So far it seems there were few people going about their business at that time of night.'

James West told the meeting that they were waiting for the pathologist to reveal officially the cause of Felicity Strutt's death.

But Tilly noticed that Miles didn't appear to be concentrating. There was sadness in his eyes; she hoped his disconsolate look didn't mean the case was becoming too much for him and he was afraid of letting down Daisy's family.

She resolved to do everything she could to find out who could have killed Daisy and why — even if she had to break the odd regulation to do it.

32

Bryson Higgins posed in front of the bathroom mirror, making minute rearrangements to his gelled hair, ensuring the spikes were in exactly the right place. He liked what he saw.

His designer T-shirt was tight and showed that the hours he'd spent in the gym had paid off. He completed the look with expensive jeans and stylish, colourful shoes. Not the attire you'd expect a computer data inputter for a district council to wear – but Higgins had taken what he deemed to be a boring job because it was all he could get after being released from prison.

He'd spent two years behind bars for assaulting a former partner, his uncontrollable rage and his insatiable appetite for women getting him into trouble on several occasions.

When he'd lashed out at his girlfriend, knocking her over and causing her to gash her head on a coffee table, she decided she couldn't take any more of his unreasonable behaviour and called the police.

While serving his sentence Higgins attended an anger management course and learned to control his violent urges. He was fortunate that the classes had recently been reinstated. A former Labour Home Secretary had decided the courses were counterproductive but the current Justice Secretary had reversed the measure.

The fact that Higgins had sought help led to his being offered a job by a council. The work was relatively well-paid, it didn't cause him any stress and it would do until he could either get something better or set up his own business.

'Bryson! Hurry up or you'll be late for work!'

His current partner's shout annoyed him but he told himself to stay cool. 'Shurrup,' he muttered as he guided a loose hair into its correct place.

He walked downstairs, grabbed a jacket that would protect him from the impending rain without damaging his appearance and opened the front door. 'See you later,' he called and almost bumped into Tilly Johnson as she was about to knock on the door.

'Bryson Higgins?'

'Who wants to know?'

Tilly knew she shouldn't have gone there alone but she was desperate to solve Daisy's murder. She introduced herself and showed her warrant card. 'Can I come in?'

'It's not convenient right now. I'm off to work.'

'Well, this can't wait. We can either have a chat here or you can come down to the station and we'll do it there.'

Tilly noticed a change in Higgins' behaviour.

'Okay, what's this all about?'

Tilly stared at him, watching for any sign that he might become violent or try to get away.

'Your ex-partner, Daisy. She's been murdered.'

Higgins took a step back. Horror engulfed his face; Tilly thought his shock was genuine.

'Now, is there anywhere we can go or should we do this in front of your partner?'

A woman in her mid-twenties wearing a low-cut top and shorts appeared out of the kitchen.

'It's okay, babe, nothing for you to worry about.'

Higgins showed Tilly into an untidy living room with remnants of the previous evening's takeaway adorning a scratched coffee table. A glass ashtray was full of cigarette ends, a lingering smell making Tilly feel uncomfortable.

'You say Daisy's been murdered?'

'Yes. Two nights ago. Where were you then?'

'I was here. All night. My partner will vouch for me. How did Daisy die?'

'Sorry. Can't tell you that.'

'Why would anyone want to kill her?'

'I thought you might know that.'

'Me? I haven't seen her for yonks.'

'When was the last time you saw her?'

Higgins hesitated. 'Must have been seven or eight years ago.'

'Are you trying to tell me you've never seen your son?'

'The stupid cow said she was on the pill. Not long afterwards told me she was pregnant. She knew all along I didn't want kids. I told her to get rid of it but she flatly refused. Not long afterwards I broke it off. Never seen her since.'

Tilly wondered why Daisy had become involved with Higgins. He didn't seem her type. Perhaps he could turn on the charm like a light switch and illuminate women's lives. She knew there was no way Higgins could press himself on her.

'Maybe you had a change of heart. For some reason you thought you'd like to get involved in your son's life, become a proper dad to him. The only way that could happen was if Daisy wasn't around.'

'I'd sooner shove a hot poker in my eye,' Bryson said. The vitriol in his voice was unmistakeable. 'Kids stop you from living your life the way you want to. Would I kill Daisy so that I could get to my son? Never heard such a load of crap in all my life.'

Tilly thought he was hiding something.

'I've looked at your record and it's not good. Two years inside for hitting your ex-partner. I reckon you've got an old-fashioned idea about women: the best place for them is in the bedroom. Or the kitchen.

'I don't know what your relationship's like with your current girlfriend. Does she think the sun shines out of your arse?'

Tilly knew she might be clutching at straws but she ploughed on. 'Does she know you go off with other women when you're supposed to be out with your mates? Perhaps you weren't here on the night Daisy was killed. Maybe you think your girlfriend loves you so much she'd give you an alibi.'

Tilly paused and looked straight at Higgins.

'Or did Daisy contact you and say she wanted money? Was that it? Was she struggling and felt you ought to be making a contribution towards your son's upkeep? Wouldn't take much for you to lose your temper and commit murder if someone pushed your far enough.'

Higgins gritted his teeth but then composed himself.

'As you must know, I went on an anger management course when I was inside. I learned to control my temper. I don't need to resort to violence any more.'

Tilly stared at him for several seconds without speaking. Then she turned and walked out of the house.

She didn't think Higgins had anything to do with Daisy's death. But she doubted whether he was at home on the night Daisy died. And she came to the conclusion that he was undoubtedly a nasty piece of work.

33

Miles' phone rang. He pulled it out of his pocket and read the display: Stuart Bainbridge.

'Hi, Stuart. What's up?'

'I presume you've seen the latest crime figures. Have you had time to digest them properly yet?'

'I've just looked at the main points. Got two big cases on my hands so I haven't got much time for reading.'

'Let me fill you in. Drug dealing: up. Car thefts: up. Shoplifting: up. Burglaries: up. One report says the public think the police have given up investigating house burglaries. And the burglars themselves don't think they'll ever be caught.

'Seems the only things being investigated are murders and offensive comments on social media. Lawlessness is running riot. Just heard some politician on the radio saying we're descending into anarchy.'

Miles took a second to think about his response: 'I joined the police to catch criminals and deter others from taking up a life of crime. The statistics might change – but not the reason why I come to work every day. You should know that – you worked with me long enough.'

'I was reading the other day about some of the new recruits joining not just your force but all constabularies. They don't know what the job's about and they're being sent out without the appropriate training. They'll be lucky if they turn into half the officer you are.'

'Very kind of you to say that.'

'And what's happening with some of these events the police are going to? Should be keeping law and order but they're dancing at Pride festivals and painting their faces to show solidarity with the public. What happened to respect for the uniform? It's just not there any more.

'Which brings me on to that proposition I put to you. Have you had chance to – '

'No, been too busy trying to catch criminals.'

'Why don't you jack it in and join me? No late nights, no early mornings, no red tape. You could spend more time with Jordan. And with Tilly.'

'Tilly? What do you mean?'

'It's pretty obvious she's crazy about you. And I reckon you feel the same about her. Think of all the romantic evenings you could have together. It's a no-brainer to me.'

Miles had found Bainbridge's job offer intriguing – but it was an unwelcome distraction. He needed to give his full attention to the two investigations and not be sidetracked by something which after all might not happen.

'Must go, Stuart. I'll be in touch.'

Alessandra de Villiers made a slight adjustment to her purple Chanel suit, then stepped into her Jimmy Choos which made her a couple of inches taller. She added the final touch: her dark-framed Gucci glasses which most people agreed gave her an extra level of sexiness.

Her long, dark brown, glossy hair framed her round face. Her large eyes and thick eyelashes offset her large, aquiline nose which she wasn't sure whether she'd inherited from her Greek mother or her French father.

What she did know was that she was grateful to her mum for passing on her sense of style and her dad for a strong work ethic and passion for life's luxuries.

Her father, a commercial pilot, and her mother, a university professor, were disappointed when she said she wanted to study law in England. But she was so resolute that they didn't stand in her way.

She decided against enrolling at Oxford, Cambridge or one of the London universities. Instead she opted for the law school at Nottingham Trent University. She was drawn to the city by its lively social scene and cultural attractions but she was careful to maintain a balance between studying and enjoying herself. It paid off as she achieved a first-class honours degree and had law firms queuing up to offer her a job.

She quickly gained respect for the way she represented her clients and there was no shortage of petty criminals anxious to have her plead on their behalf in the magistrates' court.

But although she was polite and sometimes charming, she could be blunt and direct. Some of the people in the justice system she came into contact with considered her to be snooty, even arrogant. It led to her being known as Vicious Villiers, a nickname that didn't bother her because she realised she was doing an effective job.

Today it was her firm's turn on the police station duty solicitors' rota. Anyone who'd been arrested on suspicion of committing a crime could ask for a duty solicitor who would be brought in before the suspect was interviewed.

Alessandra loved going into a police station to meet a new client. Often she didn't know the details of a case and might not have experience of dealing with the type of charge the person was facing. But she regarded that as an opportunity to increase her knowledge which would help her to become a better lawyer.

She was looking forward to whatever the day might bring – and putting the police in their place if they tried to take liberties with the people who were her clients.

34

'Helen, lovely to hear your voice again.'

'Hi, Tony. This is a nice surprise.'

'How are you – bearing up?'

'Yeah, I'm okay, thanks. Have good and bad days. Today's been good so far.'

'It's about to get much better. Are you a fan of the theatre?'

The question caught Helen unawares.

'It's not somewhere I go very often. Tend to be a movie fan rather than a theatre person.'

'Well, I've got a treat for you. I've got two tickets for a touring production of *Hamlet* that's in Nottingham this week. Do you know much about Shakespeare?'

'Not really. Always struggled with him at school. Didn't know what he was talking about half the time.'

'Ah, another victim of the British educational system. I can't understand how so many teachers get their jobs when they know so little about our national playwright. Mind you, I've seen professional productions where the actors just say their lines without giving any indication that they know what the words mean.

'But the performance we're going to see won't be anything like that. There's a clever young director who's behind it – he's influenced by the great Peter Brook.

'I was gutted when Brook died. He did have a good innings though. Ninety-six when he went to that great theatre in the sky. I don't think the UK really appreciated his talents, which is why he moved to Paris.

'I saw a documentary on television about *Hamlet*. Brook said the four most important words in the text are "taint not thy mind". That's what the Ghost of Hamlet's father tells Hamlet when he says the prince should take revenge. I'm sure you know that old Hamlet was murdered by his brother so that he could become king.

'You know, so many people in the theatre get that wrong. They reckon Hamlet was the man who couldn't make up his mind. So hopefully that will come out in this new production. Tickets are like gold dust – but I've managed to get us a couple.'

There was no response from Helen.

'And that's not all. Afterwards I've got us a table at Sat Bains' restaurant. You know who he is, don't you?'

Helen sounded perplexed. 'He's the guy with two Michelin stars, isn't he? Got a place on Lenton Lane. I've never been there – couldn't possibly afford it.'

'Don't worry about that. Sat's a personal friend of mine. They should be full but he's got a table with our name on it.'

Helen groaned.

'Something wrong?'

She had to pluck up courage before going on.

'I can't eat late at night. I just don't digest my food quickly and if I eat after about eight o'clock I can't get to sleep for ages. And I'm rubbish for most of the next day.'

'You'll be fine. What else would you be doing on an evening during the week? Nothing.'

'Well, I'd arranged to meet a girlfriend. Haven't seen her for a long time.'

'Call it off. You've got a better offer. She'll be okay with it.'

How do you know how she'll react, Helen thought. Tony had never met her friend. Helen didn't like changing arrangements at the last minute. She hoped her friend wouldn't object.

'I'll pick you up at six, then we'll be able to have a couple of drinks before the theatre. And Helen? Wear something nice, won't you?'

35

Alessandra de Villiers felt a surge of excitement as she pulled into the custody suite car park, unbuckled her seat belt and looked in her rear-view mirror to ensure her hair was in place.

She got out of her jet-black Mazda MX-5 and wondered how long it had been since she'd been able to drive it with the top down. When she bought the car she regretted the fact that it didn't come in an electric version as she was keen to do her bit to help the environment. But she forgot all about being eco-friendly whenever she got behind the wheel. She'd never experienced such exhilaration.

She was almost as delighted to be meeting a new client. From the scant details she'd been given, this could prove to be an extremely challenging yet rewarding case.

'Good morning, Miss de Villiers.' The custody sergeant greeted her with respect although she'd annoyed him with some of her outrageous demands when representing other prisoners.

'How may I help you?'

'William Montgomery Phillips. I'm here to represent him.'

'Okay. He was arrested on suspicion of murdering Felicity Strutt. We have CCTV footage of him on a bus with a suitcase which was found to contain Ms Strutt's torso. He's been examined by a nurse and a mental health team. They say he's fit to be interviewed. We'll take him to one of the consultation booths. You can talk to him there.'

Billy was sitting in a small, claustrophobic space which could accommodate two people. He was on one side, the door behind him locked. Alessandra de Villiers walked in and sat opposite him.

'Hello. My name's Alessandra.' Her tone immediately put him at ease although he felt restricted by the cramped surroundings.

'Shall I call you William or do you prefer Billy?'

'Whatever. Billy's fine.'

'I realise this is an ordeal for you but we must be careful that we don't give the police too much ammunition before your case comes to court. I'm on your side. I need you to trust me. Let's work together on this. I'm determined to do my best for you.'

Phillips found that her warm, soft voice had a calming influence on him. He sat back on his chair and relaxed.

She went on: 'Are you up for telling me what happened, how you met Felicity?'

Phillips looked up to the ceiling, then locked eyes with Alessandra. 'It started one weekend. I was watching the local news on television. That's when I first noticed Felicity. She was absolutely gorgeous.

'I thought she might want to be my girlfriend. Since my mum died I've been living on my own. The house is plenty big enough and I thought I could get her to come round and spend some time with me. Perhaps we could have a future together.'

Alessandra watched him closely, making sure her face didn't show any disbelief.

'I discovered her work email address and wrote to her, suggesting that we went on a date. She didn't even bother to reply.'

Hardly surprising, Alessandra reckoned, but nodded for him to continue.

'When she rejected me I knew I had to make her pay.'

He looked down, the colour having drained from his face as he spoke.

'So, Billy, what did you do?'

'I started hanging around the television studio. I was careful not to be spotted. You see, I've seen all these programmes about private detectives and how they conceal themselves so that the person they're following doesn't spot them. I stayed in the shadows, made sure no one saw me.

'Then early one evening I saw Felicity leaving work. I watched her get into her car – a flash red Mercedes. I thought: how can she afford one of those?

'A couple of nights later I drove my mum's car to the television station and followed Felicity when she left. She spent a couple of hours in a restaurant with some bloke who I'd never seen before. I saw them later laughing and joking. I thought: what's he got that I haven't? And why did she want to spend time with him and not with me?

'Anyway, I thought she'd go home after that but no, she drove off up Mansfield Road and parked her car in a side street. Walked to a hotel nearby. I parked not far away.

'About an hour later she came out with a big smile on her face. Made her look even more beautiful. I just couldn't take any more. Why wouldn't she let me make her happy? I grabbed her from behind and she began to struggle. I didn't want to hurt her but I didn't want anyone coming out of their house to see what all the noise was about.'

Alessandra was becoming more and more wrapped up in Phillips' story. 'Go on.'

'She was screaming at the top of her voice, so I pulled a spanner out of my pocket. I always carry it with me, you know – there are some really weird people on the streets these days. Felicity went out like a light. I only gave her a little tap. Fortunately, as I found out later, she wasn't too badly hurt. So I bundled her into the back of my mum's car and took her to my place. I couldn't have her trying to escape from me, so I handcuffed her to the spare bed.

'For the next few days I made her dinner and tried to look after her but she was so unreasonable. Kept saying "let me go, let me go". I said I couldn't do that; we were meant to be together and if I allowed her to leave she wouldn't come back.

'One day she kept going on and on about calling the police as soon as she got free. In the end I picked up the bedside lamp and hit her with it. She went quiet.

'I didn't mean to hit her that hard. But I could tell she was dead. She had a staring look in her eyes and she was lifeless.

'I couldn't tell anyone what I'd done. I didn't want the ambulance or the police coming round. Everyone knew what a wonderful woman my mother was and if they knew what I'd done, they'd think she hadn't brought me up properly. I couldn't allow her memory to be tarnished.'

Alessandra gave him a sympathetic look.

'I thought that if I could chop up her body I could get rid of it and no one would be any wiser. I used to work in an abattoir so I knew how to dismember a body. Well, I'd cut up animals, so I thought it couldn't be much different cutting up a person.

'I cut Felicity's arms and legs off. And her head. I put them in the freezer. I was going to get rid of them after I'd disposed of the torso but the police came and arrested me.

'I can't go to prison, I just can't. Please help me!'

Alessandra was beginning to formulate a plan that she thought might just work.

'All right. I'll do everything I can. For the time being, Billy, when the police interview you, make sure you say "no comment" to every question.'

36

Tony Goodson kept a thick, detailed file of most of the East Midlands' notorious criminals. He picked it up to refresh his memory.

Only two murderers in the area fulfilled the criteria of what was generally accepted as a serial killer: ending the life of three or more people, with the murders having a significant period of time between them.

But Goodson knew that some so-called experts disagreed: the FBI described criminals who'd murdered only two people as serial killers while others maintained that there had to be four victims for the epithet of serial killer to be justified.

Goodson knew Nottinghamshire had only ever had one recognised serial killer: Mark Martin who was dubbed 'the Sneinton Strangler'. Born in Ilkeston, just over the Derbyshire border, he befriended alcoholics and drug addicts who were homeless. He killed three young women whose ages ranged from eighteen to twenty-six. It happened between 2004 and 2005.

He was believed to be the only Nottinghamshire criminal who was sentenced to a whole life order – meaning he will never be released. Goodson had seen his story immortalised in the television true crime series *Britain's Most Evil Killers.*

Goodson also knew that Dr Harold Shipman, who was given a life sentence in 2000 for murdering fifteen of his patients, was born in Sherwood in Nottinghamshire – but he didn't commit any of his crimes in the county.

Goodson then looked at what had happened in Derbyshire. Twenty-six-year-old Michael Copeland, a former soldier, confessed to murdering three men in 1960 and 1961. He allegedly killed them because he suspected they might be gay and he hated homosexuals.

Goodson re-read that two of Copeland's victims were murdered in Chesterfield: the first, William Elliott, drove a bubble car so it was known as 'the bubble car murder'. The body of the third, George Stubbs, was discovered a hundred yards from where William Elliott was found, so this became known as 'the copycat murder'.

In between, Copeland killed a sixteen-year-old youth near the barracks where Copeland was stationed in Germany. He was sentenced to death but this was commuted to life in prison after the UK abolished the death penalty.

Goodson knew that Leicestershire had never had a serial killer although Colin Pitchfork was a name that resonated with people around the world. He was the first person convicted of rape and murder using DNA profiling. He killed two fifteen-year-old girls, Lynda Mann in 1983 and Dawn Ashworth in 1986.

The police and the Forensic Science Service worked for six months to take blood samples from five-and-a-half thousand local men without finding a match to the semen found on the two girls. It was only when one of Pitchfork's work colleagues boasted that he'd taken a test while claiming to be Pitchfork that the bakery worker was arrested.

Goodson recalled that Pitchfork was sentenced to life in prison with a minimum jail term of thirty years which was reduced to twenty-eight years on appeal. He was granted parole in 2021 and released on licence but was recalled to prison for breaching his licence conditions.

The East Midlands Express occasionally took in parts of Lincolnshire, especially when a major story broke. Goodson realised there'd been few bigger stories than the case of Beverley Allitt, otherwise known as 'the angel of death'.

The nurse at Grantham and Kesteven Hospital was convicted of murdering four children, attempting to murder three others and causing grievous bodily harm to another six in 1991. She was the only nurse on duty when all the children were attacked.

Her motive was never explained although one theory suggested she suffered from Munchausen syndrome by proxy which 'involves a carer making a dependent person mentally or physically ill in order to gain attention'. A likely story, Goodson thought.

Allitt was sentenced to thirteen concurrent terms of life imprisonment. Although two leading experts concluded that Allitt wasn't mentally ill, she was sent to Rampton Secure Hospital in Nottinghamshire to serve her sentence.

Goodson put the file back into his drawer where he kept his personal documents in the study of his home in one of the middle-class areas of Nottingham. Everything was in its place, arranged methodically so that it took Goodson only seconds before he could put his hands on exactly what he wanted.

With his mother's health failing and no other family members to take care of her, Goodson had sold his flat in the city centre and moved in with her. She enjoyed his working from home although he often went out to talk to contacts or to dig around for stories that none of his colleagues knew about.

'I'm going out for a bit, mum. I won't be long.'

His mother was silent; she didn't even grunt as he went out.

He thought about the day ahead: he was going to court for the first appearance of William Montgomery Phillips, accused of the murder of Felicity Strutt.

Would Phillips go down in history as one of Nottinghamshire's most infamous criminals? Or would it turn out that he was even more notorious and would become only the county's second serial killer? He could hardly wait to hear all the grisly details.

37

For more than a quarter of a century anyone charged with a criminal offence in Nottingham made their first appearance at the city's magistrates' court. It was built on the site of the old Carrington Street railway station, with the Midland Railway goods shed being turned into a car park.

Pre-1996 court cases were heard in the Guildhall and the Shire Hall. Both were then closed, with the Shire Hall being converted into the Galleries of Justice which later changed its name to the National Justice Museum.

The new magistrates' court complex comprised twenty-four court rooms which dealt with everything from motoring offences to minor assaults. Justices of the Peace handled ninety-five per cent of all criminal cases although indictable offences including murder, manslaughter and robbery were sent to the Crown Court for trial or sentencing.

Miles walked into the building at 9.30am, the time by which anyone charged with a criminal offence had to arrive to ensure they didn't breach their bail conditions.

He noticed several faces he knew well, petty criminals who were regular attenders at court, the majority of them unconcerned that their indiscretions had again been uncovered.

There were others he couldn't identify, their casual clothing and blustering manner emphasising how little respect they had for the law and the court process. Miles smiled to himself when he thought they'd be put in their place by one of the court clerks who simply wouldn't accept their impudence.

He nodded to a couple of uniformed officers who'd be called to give evidence in cases where they'd made an arrest.

The first officer, a bearded, middle-aged man whose arms were covered in tattoos, was composed and slightly bored. He knew that the court process often meant hanging around outside the actual courtroom waiting for his case to be called.

The other constable, a much younger man who was clean-shaven and whose uniform looked immaculate, couldn't keep still. There was a hint of fear and desperation in his eyes; this would be his first time in the witness box.

'Good morning, Detective Inspector.' Miles, concentrating on putting names to faces, was taken aback when he heard his name. He turned around.

'Good morning, Miss de Villiers. Nice to see you again.'

'You *can* call me Alesssandra, you know.'

She was dressed in her customary two-piece suit with a white, elegant blouse, designer glasses and high heels.

'I hope you're not going to surprise us with anything unexpected this morning, are you?'

Alessandra feigned a look of hurt. 'As if I'd do anything like that. On a remand hearing.'

'I hear you're representing Billy Phillips. Nice man, from all accounts.' Miles regretted the sarcasm which he couldn't disguise in his voice.

She put her hand on his arm. 'Let's just say he wouldn't be the sort of man I'd take home to have tea with my parents. They would of course be delighted to meet someone like you.'

The remark threw Miles. He liked Alesssandra. A lot. He never referred to her as Vicious Villiers because he felt she didn't deserve the nickname – all she was doing was representing her clients in the best possible way.

Was she propositioning him?

He dismissed the thought. It was just banter between two people who'd been thrown together in the course of their work. But the remark stayed with him.

'I understand that Mr Phillips has been declared fit to plead.'

'That's correct. But of course you know there's a huge difference between fitness to plead and fitness to stand trial. I'll be arranging for a complete mental health assessment of my client before I make my submissions.'

'And we'll be conducting our own examination too.'

Half an hour later Phillips walked up the steps from a cell underneath the courtroom. He looked bewildered as the clerk of the court read out the charges he was facing: kidnap and murder.

The prosecutor, a dapper, upright man in his forties with slicked-back hair and a goatee beard, outlined the essential facts of the case.

'In view of the seriousness of the offences, the prosecution will be applying to remand the defendant in custody to await trial at the Crown Court.'

Alessandra de Villiers jumped to her feet. Miles thought she might come up with something he hadn't bargained for in an attempt to get the charges dismissed. But all she said was: 'No application for bail at this stage.'

38

Helen Loudon woke with a start. Having a bad dream. But as soon as her eyes opened she'd forgotten the details. She knew it was something unpleasant but no matter how hard she tried she couldn't recall what had caused her heart rate to soar.

Not that she'd slept much. She just couldn't put out of her mind Tony Goodson's plans for their night out together. It wasn't the Shakespeare that bothered her – she was capable of looking engrossed in a play even if she didn't have a clue what it meant.

It was the whole event she was worried about: drinks before the show, probably in a bar that she'd never frequented and where she'd feel uncomfortable; the theatre itself because she hadn't been in one since she was a giggly teenager with her classmates; and then the incredibly classy restaurant where she was sure she'd make a fool of herself, spilling her drink or showing Tony up with her eating habits. She knew she was overthinking what might happen but it was gnawing at her brain incessantly. How could she get out of it?

She lay on the bed, the duvet thrown back despite the chilly evening as she sweated over the problem. Thinking, thinking.

Thinking.

She'd just have to tell him she couldn't make it. Maybe the friend she told Tony she was going out with had taken ill. Yes, that's it. Her friend had developed some horrible disease, lived on her own and there was no one else to look after her. Couldn't get up, needed someone to make her cups of tea, hadn't got any shopping in.

But would Tony believe her? Probably not. She didn't care anyway – she just wasn't going. As much as she liked Tony, she didn't want him dictating her movements and what time she'd be allowed home.

She looked at the clock: 7am. She picked up her phone. Should she call him? She hadn't found out enough about him to know whether he was a night owl or an early bird. He could be up and about already. She couldn't face it if she told him she wasn't accompanying him on his night out and he berated her. No, she'd text him.

She wrote a message, read it three times – and put her phone down.

She went downstairs, made a cup of tea and went back to her bedroom. She checked the message, hoping it came across in the way she intended, and pressed the "send" button.

She lay back, her head on the pillow. Less than a minute later she was startled as she heard her ringtone. The display said: Tony.

Her body shook with fear. If she'd have wanted to answer it she couldn't – she was fixed to the spot. After a few seconds which seemed to go on interminably, the ringing stopped.

Helen tried to relax. Her heart which had been thumping at an alarming rate started to slow down. She exhaled, sighed and felt a wave of relief all at once.

But the rate shot up again when she heard a ping signifying she had a voicemail. It had to be Tony.

Her hand shook as she accessed the message. 'Helen, what's going on? Sending me a text to tell me you're not coming – it's just not on. Fortunately for you I'll be able to let someone else have the theatre tickets.

'But I can't understand why you wouldn't want to go to the most exclusive restaurant for miles around. There's usually a list of people waiting to get a table there. Sat is a good friend of mine – I'll speak to him to cancel. Hopefully he'll be okay with that. I just hope the next time I want a table, he'll be able to squeeze me in.

'I've got to go – my news editor wants to brief me on the story I'm covering for today's front page. But I'm not happy, Helen. I'll call you in a day or two to fix something else up. And I won't take no for an answer. Don't ever stand me up like that again.'

39

'Alessandra! Great to hear from you. It's been a while.'

'So it has, John. Sorry I've not been in touch lately. But I think I've got something that could be right up your street.'

John Huntingdon was a forensic psychologist who was often contacted by both prosecution and defence lawyers when they needed an expert witness. He'd worked with Alessandra on a couple of cases which had both gone in her favour. The only reason she hadn't called on his services lately had nothing to do with his talents – she'd been dealing with criminals whose mental health hadn't been called into question.

Huntingdon, a slim, tall man in his fifties, had a full head of hair which had turned grey. Yet his moustache and beard were jet black, giving him an eccentric look. He tried to make himself appear younger by wearing expensive, up-to-date clothes which were elegant and caught most people's attention.

With a string of letters after his name, he possessed the knowledge that made him a respected expert in his field. Add to that an unshakeable belief in himself and you had someone who could always present a strong argument in the witness box.

'Okay, how can I help?'

Alessandra told him about Billy Phillips and the charges he was facing. 'What do you reckon?'

'Sounds like it could be a case of manslaughter by reason of diminished responsibility.'

'I was hoping you might say that.'

'What you must remember, though, is that manslaughter isn't a silver bullet. It might lead to a reduced sentence – but it could still mean your client could spend many years in prison.'

'I realise that. But I don't think Billy deserves to spend the rest of his days in jail. Will you do an assessment on him?'

Miles made himself a strong cup of coffee as he prepared to go through anything that had come in overnight. He was hoping for new leads and always tried to retain an optimistic mood although sometimes positivity gave way to realism as investigations stalled.

He'd hardly started to make inroads into the paperwork when his phone rang. A detective inspector who'd been on duty overnight didn't bother with any small talk.

'Miles, someone got in touch in the early hours about the Daisy Higgins case. Said he was at a dinner a couple of nights before she was murdered. This guy didn't leave his name. Said he'd been for a leak and on his way back from the toilet he saw two blokes acting furtively. He thought Daisy had overheard the end of their conversation and they didn't look at all pleased.'

Miles perked up straightaway. 'What sort of dinner was it?'

'It was the annual gathering of some business organisation. The guy didn't name it but I'm sure you'll be able to find out whose it was.'

'Any description of the two men?'

'No, the guy rang off before we could get any more info out of him.'

Miles cursed under his breath. 'Anything else?'

'Only that Daisy went up to another man who suddenly appeared. The caller said he put his arms around her and comforted her. The most remarkable thing about this new fella was that he was very tall – huge, the caller described him.'

Time for another word with Cameron White, Miles thought.

As his team started to arrive ready for the morning briefing, Miles' phone rang again. This time it was the control room inspector.

'Miles, we've got another body. It's definitely one for you. A young woman, found in the water – and her fingers have been cut off.'

40

Tilly accompanied Miles who drove as fast as possible to the crime scene. It was back in Derby, within walking distance of his home. The River Derwent ran near his street which was populated by former railway workers' cottages. They were close enough to the station to encourage residents to use the train – if staff weren't on strike.

The riverside path linked the Bass Recreation Ground – bequeathed to the city by benefactor and brewery boss Michael Bass – to the Pride Park business area. Miles would often see thousands of football fans taking the National Cycle Network path number six to Pride Park Stadium on match days, their black-and-white colours signifying they were supporters of Derby County, one of the twelve original members of the Football League which began in 1888.

But all he could see now was the blue and white of the police tape which ensured that no one could get close enough to look at what they might regard as a distressing scene.

'Oh, Tilly, nearly forgot. When you've got a minute, please call the Storm and find out when they're training over the next couple of days. We need to have another chat with

Cameron White. There might be something about Daisy's death that he's forgotten to tell us.'

A CSI team had already erected a tent on the towpath and had begun a meticulous search for forensic evidence. Miles and Tilly pulled on white oversuits as they prepared to inspect the body.

'Do you reckon Daisy's killer has struck again?' Tilly's question had more than a sense of inevitability.

'We'll soon know,' said Miles, hiding the trepidation and nervousness that he was experiencing.

They walked slowly towards a railway bridge, taking in everything around them, before getting their first glimpse of the body.

Miles recoiled, shock and recognition etched on his face.

'Do you know her?'

'I'm afraid so, Tilly. It's Alessandra de Villiers.'

Back at police HQ, Miles' brain was overheating. So many theories were scattering around his head, so many questions were unanswered. Who hated Alessandra enough to kill her – a criminal who thought he or she hadn't been given a fair trial? What was she doing near the canal? Where was her car? Did the killer follow her or was it a random killing? Did

Alessandra know Daisy? Did they have a common enemy who was ruthless enough to end their lives?

He went in search of coffee – and was astounded to see Alessandra's photo on the front page of the East Midlands Express.

Tony Goodson's name was even bigger than usual just beneath a headline which proclaimed **Knife crime: 'too many' deaths**.

Miles knew the story had been written to achieve maximum impact as well as sell more newspapers.

Bereaved relatives have called for more action from the police after the number of victims of knife crime reached a record high.

And the families recruited the services of top lawyer Alessandra de Villiers after she revealed she lost a close friend who was stabbed to death.

At a meeting in a Derby pub last night Ms De Villiers said she was still heartbroken following the death four months ago of her friend Josh Smith.

Josh was walking home after a night out when he was set upon by a gang. He didn't know any of them. They were drunk and looking for trouble.

Josh tried to walk away but they wouldn't let him. One of them pulled out a knife. Josh didn't stand a chance. He bled to death.'

Ms de Villiers was close to tears as she recalled how her friend died on the street.

'Someone called the police but they took far too long to respond. By the time they got there the gang had disappeared. And no one's been able to identify them.

'What are the police doing about knife crime? Obviously not enough. Not a weekend goes by without someone losing their life to a knife. We need more action.'

Ms de Villiers' comments come as figures from the Office of National Statistics show that the number of serious offences across Derbyshire involving a knife in a calendar year passed the one thousand mark for the first time.

Detective Superintendent Tom Brooksby told the meeting that knife crime was a priority for East Midlands Police because it had a 'devastating' effect on communities as well as individuals.

He said: 'We want to get knives off the streets and stop people joining gangs.

'It's about education, letting youngsters know about the consequences of carrying a blade so they can make the right choice in the first place.'

Det Supt Brooksby stressed that several initiatives were helping to bring down the number of knife attacks.

'We've got extra patrols on the streets, metal-detecting knife arches in areas that we've recognised as hot spots and dedicated knife-crime teams.

'Some of these measures have been introduced in the past few weeks but I can assure everyone we're working all year round to bring down knife crime.'

However, Ms de Villiers was unimpressed.

'I have little confidence that the police's actions will have any effect. We need stronger deterrents so that people don't even think about picking up a knife. Even one death from a knife is one too many.'

Miles thought Alessandra's closing thoughts were a little unfair – it was the government, not the police, who were responsible for deterrents. But he agreed that the law should be looked at and tightened up.

He thought Brooksby had handled himself well and defended the force as best he could. Miles was also grateful that he'd had nothing to do with the team looking after knife crime so the Chief Constable wouldn't have another excuse to have a go at him.

Did someone at that meeting take exception to Alessandra's comments? Miles thought most of the people at the meeting would probably agree with her about one death being one too many. But who would want to take her life?

Could it be the same person who murdered Daisy? He threw the paper onto the floor as he struggled to control his anger.

41

Miles was eager to get the early-evening briefing under way so that his team could try to unmask Daisy's and Alessandra's killer or killers.

'Okay, listen up. We've now got an extra case to investigate. Some of you know Alessandra de Villiers, the solicitor. You might have been on the wrong end of her questioning when you've been giving evidence in court. Well, that won't happen again – she's dead.

'Her body was found in the River Derwent in Derby earlier today and her fingers had been removed. We're waiting to hear the cause of death.

'Now the only thing we know for sure is that Billy Phillips couldn't have done it – he's tucked up in a cell.

'We need to find out as soon as we can whether the same person killed both women. Uniform are speaking to all the people who were at the meeting last night when Alessandra slagged us off for not doing enough to prevent knife crime. Was anyone there who disagreed with Alessandra? Maybe it was someone the knife-crime team were looking at in relation to another attack.

'We also need to find out whether anyone connected to Daisy was acquainted with Alessandra.

'Tilly, can you throw any more light on what happened to Daisy?'

Tilly looked nervous as she prepared to update the team.

'Boss, I've been in touch with Derby Storm. They've told me about a dinner a few days ago when Daisy might have overheard something she shouldn't. That's the next thing to check.

'I also asked when we can have a chat with Cameron White. He might be able to tell us a bit more about what happened that evening. But we can definitely rule him out of Alessandra's death.'

'Oh? How's that?'

'Before Alessandra died, he left the country. The Storm say he's gone to Syria.'

It was the beginning of the afternoon when Tilly picked up the phone to ring Cameron White. She'd checked the time: Syria was three hours ahead of the UK. If White was playing basketball while he was out there, this might be a good time to call him.

She dialled the number that the Storm had given her, a hotel in Damascus, and was put through to White's room.

It took a while for him to answer, a groggy voice indicating he'd just woken up.

'Mr White, it's DC Tilly Johnson from the East Midlands Police. Sorry to disturb you.'

'I was just having a nap. Before today's game. I'm playing for a Syrian team in a pre-season tournament. Tip-off's in a couple of hours.'

'I wish you'd told us you were leaving the country. We're right in the middle of a murder investigation.'

'Came up unexpectedly. My agent called. Said the guy I was replacing had turned his ankle in practice and would be out for several weeks. I just had time to throw a few things in a suitcase and hop on a plane.'

'Bit strange, isn't it, your employers releasing you to go and play for someone else?'

White, now sounding fully awake, had a hint of arrogance as he replied: 'I think it's a clever move on their part. I'm only here for a week, I'll miss one Storm game and then I'll be back to show everyone in Britain what a great player I am. And while I'm here I'm making really good money. No one in your country can compete with that. I was the best player on the court in my first game over here, so I expect there'll be a lot of ball clubs making me offers for next season. It's a win-win situation for everyone.'

Not for everyone at the Storm who are expecting loyalty from their players, Tilly thought. She acknowledged White's abilities on court but she was losing respect for the American as a person. Despite that she knew he might be able to shed some light on what had happened to Daisy.

'Now then, let me take you back to an evening before Daisy died. A dinner at the Storm Centre. Do you recall it?'

'I remember being there. I forget whose event it was but the organisation wanted a couple of Storm players to be there and talk to the guests. Naturally, as captain, I was one of the players.'

'And did you witness anything . . . unusual?'

'Unusual? What exactly do you mean?'

Tilly was losing her patience with White and was struggling to control her temper.

'Was Daisy upset at all?'

White was silent for a few seconds.

'Well, she came up to me towards the end of the evening and said she'd overheard a couple of guys talking. She said she only caught the tail end of their conversation but she thought they were arranging a drugs deal or something.'

'How did that affect Daisy?'

'She was really worried. I told her to forget about it. She was concerned that this was going on at the Storm and might reflect badly on her employers.'

'Did you see these two men?'

'From a distance.'

'Would you recognise them if you saw them again?'

'I doubt it. I just had a quick look, then Daisy wanted me to give her a hug.'

'Was she the sort of person who let things get to her?'

'Absolutely not. She was level-headed, intelligent – she was one cool lady. I thought at the time she might have been overreacting. Afterwards I realised I should have paid more attention to her but by then it was too late.'

Exasperated, Tilly sighed at White's recollection of events.

'Mr White, why didn't you tell us this when we spoke to you previously?'

'Well, I didn't think it was important. I'd got other things on my mind. The Storm's next game for one thing. I suppose you could say I'm obsessed with basketball. And now I'd like to concentrate on playing for my new team in Damascus. We've got a great chance of winning this tournament.'

'I suppose I should wish you good luck.'

'Ma'am, luck don't play no part in my game. It's time to kick ass.'

42

Miles' team assembled for the early-morning briefing and most of them appeared surprisingly upbeat even though they'd been working non-stop for more days than they cared to remember.

Miles scanned the room and noticed Paul Allen had a downcast look. He cupped his chin in his hand and refused an offer of coffee.

'What's up, Paul?'

Allen's voice sounded as though he had marbles in his cheek: 'Toothache. Been up half the night.'

'Well, it's obvious it's not wisdom teeth. You're not clever enough for those!' said Miles and instantly regretted the remark.

But the room erupted as detectives saw the tables being turned on Allen, the joker who never thought twice about getting a laugh at someone else's expense.

'Come on, guys, calm down. I know some of you were hoping to watch the rugby on TV later. But that won't be possible. We've got another murder to tackle.

'I'm fairly certain the person who killed Daisy Higgins has struck again, so we need to look into Alessandra's lifestyle, find out who she associated with. I want checks on her bank accounts, mobile phone, car, social media, everything. Where did she go last night after that meeting, the one where people were complaining that we weren't doing enough about knife crime? Did she upset anyone? Had anyone got a grudge against her because of a court case?'

James West jumped in: 'Boss, I seem to recall a case in the Crown Court a couple of years ago. Alessandra and a barrister were representing a guy who'd been caught by vigilantes grooming a young girl. I don't know if he thought he'd get a suspended sentence but the judge sent him down. This guy went crazy. Slagged off Alessandra and the barrister from the dock. He might have wanted revenge.'

'Good shout, James. Find out who this guy was and where he is now. I'm going to have a chat with Alessandra's boss.'

The village of Edwalton to the south east of Nottingham was sought after because it contained some of the area's most expensive properties. Although it comprised mainly housing estates, the wealthier people in the population of just over four thousand were able to splash the cash on highly desirable homes.

Arthur Wilkinson, head of one of Nottingham's biggest legal firms, had invested wisely as his company grew in size. The six-bedroom 'character property', as the estate agent had described it, with a south-facing rear garden, was set in half an acre of land which ensured the owner's privacy.

With a tennis court and plenty of space for other ball games, Wilkinson's four children had enjoyed living there as they grew up. But they'd now left for top jobs in other cities. Yet their parents had no intention of moving, even though they could probably sell the property for close on two million pounds.

Miles drove up the sweeping gravel drive to a large turning circle and parked facing the way out.

Wilkinson opened the front door himself. The slightly built man whose hair had almost disappeared looked anything but an eminent businessman in his checked shirt, woollen cardigan and slacks.

He showed Miles through a vast reception hall into an impressive, open-plan living room and dining kitchen which lead onto a huge patio. Perfect for idyllic summer evenings – but not for a morning like this when frost was taking far too long to clear, Miles thought.

He accepted the offer of coffee and sat down while Wilkinson switched on the Nespresso coffee machine.

There was sadness and disbelief in his eyes. 'I can't understand it. Who would want to kill Alessandra?'

'I was hoping you might tell me that.'

'I've got no idea. My firm has represented lots of criminals, obviously, some of them murderers. But I don't think any of them would kill their lawyer. I'm . . . shocked. Still haven't taken it in.'

Miles took a long drink of his coffee.

'When did you last see Alessandra?'

'Yesterday, in the office, after she came back from court.'

'How did she seem?'

'Same as always. Bright, pleasant. Everything had gone well at court, so she was in a good mood.'

Miles put his coffee cup on the worktop of the contemporary, minimalist kitchen which oozed quality and expense.

'We need to build up a picture of Alessandra's lifestyle. Was she in a relationship with anyone?'

'Not that I know of.'

'No one at work she was close to?'

'Absolutely not. That was one thing she was clear about – she'd never mix work and pleasure. She was totally driven when it came to the legal profession. We'd had chats about her possibly becoming a director of the company. I'm sure she wouldn't want to jeopardise that by getting involved with someone in the office.'

'What about previous relationships? Perhaps she ended one and that person wanted to get back at her?'

'She rarely spoke about anyone apart from her parents who she loved dearly. Went to see them as often as she could. But of course that was difficult with them living abroad.'

Miles drained his coffee before making eye contact again.

'As far as you're aware, did she have any financial problems? Maxed-out credit cards? Gambling debts?'

Wilkinson chuckled at the suggestion: 'She was known at work for keeping a tight rein on her finances. She spent a fair amount on clothes – knew she had to look good when she met clients and appeared in court. But apart from that you couldn't accuse her of being extravagant. She was always going around turning off lights and making sure all the computers were off as well.'

'Now, do you know anything about her friend Josh Smith?'

'Yes, of course, They were good mates. I think they were at university together. I met him a couple of times. Nice guy.'

Miles trod carefully with his next question: 'Were they . . . an item at any time?'

'Oh no, Josh was gay.'

'And what about the meeting Alessandra went to, when people were asking for more action on knife crime?'

Wilkinson grew angry but remained in control: 'She joined a community group who were trying everything possible to get the police to do something about the number of stabbings. She was doing that not just because of Josh but also because of her community spirit.

'She was very critical of what East Midlands Police were doing to tackle the problem. Maybe one of your officers took exception to her comments and decided to take the law into their own hands.'

43

'James, what have you got?'

'Boss, the case that I mentioned. Worse than I thought. I was waiting to give evidence in a different case but there was a delay. So I nipped into one of the other courts to see what was going on.

'Kevin Dankworth, charged with five counts including attempting to engage in sex with a child. He'd gone onto a dating app and thought he was chatting to a thirteen-year-old girl. Sent her a picture of himself with nothing on.

'He was actually talking to a member of a vigilante group. This person asked Dankworth where he lived and he foolishly revealed his address. The vigilante told his mates who all turned up at Dankworth's house.

'It got a bit fractious when the vigilantes tried to make a citizen's arrest. Thankfully someone called the cops and Dankworth was taken away.'

West looked at his notes before ploughing on.

'Dankworth had a barrister who'd been briefed well by Alessandra. The barrister came out with a brilliant speech, saying Dankworth was disgusted with his behaviour and he'd done something about it. Contacted a charity that was dedicated to preventing child sexual abuse.

'There was a bit of a sob story about how this incident had changed Dankworth's life. His wife left him and moved away – he'd had no contact with her since. He'd had to go into rented accommodation because there was so much hostility towards him from his neighbours. Lost his job too with a firm he'd worked for for thirty years. The barrister made a great case for his client. I really thought he was going to get off.'

He paused long enough for Miles to ask what happened next.

'The judge said any right-thinking person would be appalled at what Dankworth had done. He'd crossed the line, so a community order wasn't appropriate. Sent him down for 15 months.

'He went crazy after he was sentenced. Had a go at the judge, his barrister and Alessandra too. I remember at the time thinking that was a bit much – I'm sure Alessandra wouldn't have told him he'd still be walking the streets after the court case.'

Miles gave a half-smile.

'Good work, James. And where's Dankworth now?'

'Served his sentence and he's out. Doubtful that he's living anywhere in Nottinghamshire but we're searching for him to see if he returned to get his own back on Alessandra.'

Miles thanked West and asked him to continue the search for Dankworth. But he knew it was unlikely he'd killed Alessandra or Daisy. Who'd done it was still a mystery.

Miles woke with a start when the alarm went off, signalling that even though it was Sunday he had to get up. Some people regarded Sunday as a day of rest. But not Miles. He'd had to postpone a day out with his son; a murder investigation came before everything else.

He thought about Stuart Bainbridge, tucked up at home in bed, catching up on his sleep, nothing getting in the way of his leisure time at the weekend. Miles wondered whether he ought to accept his former boss's offer of a job.

Snap out of it, he chided himself. Do what you're good at – catching criminals.

After the quickest shower he'd ever had, a cup of tea and a bowl of muesli, he got into his car for what he hoped would be a quick, traffic-less journey from his home in Derby to Nottingham.

He stopped at a supermarket near police headquarters to pick up a selection of cakes for his team, anxious to keep their energy levels as high as possible as they tried to make progress on two murder investigations.

'Good morning, everyone. Where are we with our inquiries?'

James West, looking as though he'd been on a three-day pub crawl, was the first to speak.

'Felicity Strutt. The pathologist's completed the post-mortem. She was killed by a blow to the head with a blunt object. Now it's a matter of building the case against Phillips.

'As for Alessandra, her car's been found in a side street not far from the canal. It was parked a bit strange – it was almost as if another car had overtaken her and forced her into the kerb.

'We're waiting for the pathologist's report which should give us an idea of the time of death. We've also requested phone records from her provider which will tell us who was the last person she spoke to.'

West had saved the most significant information until the end.

'CCTV officers have been going through footage from near the scene and we've picked up a BMW 3 Series which pinged a camera a couple of times. At this very moment we're finding out who the car is registered to.'

'Great work, everyone. Let's keep at it.'

Tilly Johnson then revealed what she'd discovered: 'Boss, as far as we're aware, there was no connection between Daisy and Alessandra. We don't think they ever met.

'I've looked into who would benefit from their deaths. Neither of them had a huge amount of savings, so we can rule out money as a motive.

'I think we can also discount another of the usual reasons for murder – sex. Neither appeared to have a recent partner who might have been angry because they'd broken off a relationship.

'That leaves us with revenge. Possible but we haven't come across anyone yet who might have wanted retribution against either of them.'

Miles thought aloud: 'Could it be that the murderer has a lust for killing which has only recently come to the surface? Either that or he's murdered before but something stopped his killing spree. He could have left the country – or been in prison. We need to check whether anyone serving time for murder has been released recently.

'We've got to try to get into the mind of the killer. Did he just come across Daisy and Alessandra when he was out on the road at night? Or did he know they'd be at those meetings and followed them?

'I think the man we're looking for – and it probably *is* a male – wants to attract attention to himself with these killings. By cutting off his victims' fingers he's showing us he's vain, arrogant and playing a game with us.

'It appears as though we're dealing with a psychopath. He craves control and achieves that through using and abusing women before discarding them.'

A voice from the back of the room said: 'Where do you think we'll find him, boss?'

'I imagine he'll be reasonably intelligent. He obviously knows a little about forensics too.

'There probably won't be any features that mark him out as a serial killer – he'll blend into society without any problem. He'll appear to be a fairly normal guy who holds down a job. He could be living next door to any one of us.'

44

Mention Nottingham's Lenton Lane and people of a certain age recalled how it used to be the home of commercial television in the East Midlands.

Central Television's studio complex in the city opened in 1984 and was known for the efficient way it produced programmes. Sometimes the staff made twenty-six shows in two weeks – a relentless pace.

The studios became known for hosting game shows including *Bullseye,* a quiz centred on darts which became a cult classic, *The Price Is Right* in which contestants won prizes if they guessed the retail price of various products and *Supermarket Sweep,* with contestants dashing around a store trying to fill their trolley.

But the studios were closed in 2004 when there was a shake-up of independent television in the UK. The University of Nottingham acquired the site which became a vaccination centre in 2021, administering more than one thousand Covid-19 jabs a day as the government tried to get the virus under control.

In modern times other people considered Lenton Lane the place to go if they won the lottery and wanted to splash out on a car as a trademark of their new status.

As James West drove along the industrial estate he gazed at the modern showrooms housing some of the most exquisite supercars he would never get his hands on. They were gleaming despite the grey, depressing clouds which signalled yet more rain was on the way.

At one time he regularly bought a lottery ticket, hoping his numbers would come up so that he could get his hands on one of these cars that cost more than many people's home. But the longer the lottery went on and the top prize became ever more desirable, West realised his chances of winning were becoming infinitesimal, so he stopped buying tickets.

As he caught sight of a stunning, black Ferrari 812 GTS, a snip at just over three hundred and fifty thousand pounds, he thought he might have to restart his old habit of making a weekly visit to a newsagent for a ticket. He'd searched online for the model a couple of days previously when he had a few spare moments and he was astonished to see it had a top speed of 211mph (340km/h). It could accelerate from stationary to 62mph (100km/h) in only 3.8 seconds.

Then his eyes wandered to a white Maserati Grecale Trofeo, for sale at a price just below six figures.

Ah well, he mused. You wouldn't be able to drive either of them on British roads at anything approaching their top speed — unless you wanted to have a starring role in the next *Police Interceptors* TV series.

Driving further down the road, West came to a second-hand dealership which was more to his taste. There were cars of all makes and sizes, from small runabouts for drivers who'd just passed their test to luxurious models for those who had more disposable income than the average motorist.

As rain started to fall he parked his car as close to the entrance as possible.

'I'm sorry, sir. Would you mind not leaving your vehicle there? We're expecting a delivery any moment.'

A stocky man whose stomach was hanging over his trousers confronted West as soon as he got through the door. With slick-backed hair, a three-piece suit with wide pinstripes and a lairy tie, the salesman's confident exterior disappeared when West produced his warrant card.

'Er, how can I help? It's not about that parking ticket again, is it? I paid it. I'm sure I've got the receipt somewhere.'

'No. I'm afraid it's far more serious than that.'

West told him about the BMW seen on the night of Alessandra's murder that was registered to his company.

'That's impossible. It hasn't left the forecourt since it came into our possession.'

West wanted to know whether any of the staff were allowed to drive the company's cars that were for sale.

'Yes. We're like most businesses in that we give our employees permission to use our cars in the evenings and at weekends. Unless they've got points on their licence!'

He sniggered but West remained straight-faced.

'We've got an insurance policy that covers all the staff,' the salesman continued. 'If someone wants a particular car, we'll stick six months' tax on it. One of the perks of the job.'

'And no one's been driving the BMW?'

'No. It's had a few admiring glances but no one's asked to take it home yet. BMW drivers have a certain reputation. Maybe none of the staff want to be thought of like that.'

West asked for a list of the company's employees. The salesman promised to get it to him by the end of the day.

'So how do you explain the fact that the BMW was seen in the city centre last night?' asked West.

'Impossible. The car hasn't left the forecourt. We keep details of the mileage when we acquire a vehicle. Check if you like – it'll be the same. It hasn't even been out on a test drive.'

45

Helen Loudon sat down with an early-morning cup of tea and a slice of toast, trying to come to terms with how her life was shaping up. There was only one conclusion: it was time for her to go back to work.

She enjoyed her job as a project manager with a logistics company based near East Midlands Airport. She'd been there since leaving school. Her organised mind and propensity for hard work had meant she'd made quick progress to become a respected team leader who was liked by everyone.

The company had been brilliant to her when she got pregnant and during Jack's illness. When he died they never pressed her into going back to work until she was totally ready.

Although she was grateful to the firm, she didn't want to take advantage by extending her absence any longer.

But there was one thing holding her back: Tony Goodson. Since Covid her job had changed and she was needed in the office only one day a week. She could arrange everything just as easily from her home – but she doubted whether she'd be able to concentrate on her work if Tony showed up.

Maybe she could ask her bosses if she could go to the company's headquarters on a more regular basis.

But as she took a slurp of her tea she told herself that wasn't the answer. There was nothing to stop Tony appearing on her doorstep on any of the days when she was working from home. If he saw her car parked on the drive he knew she'd be in.

Was she being stupid? All she'd done was to spurn his advances when he wanted to take her out. But the message he left on her phone left her cold; it wasn't what he said but the way he said it.

She bit off a corner of her toast, still thinking hard. Should she go to the police? What good would that do? And what would she say – I think I've got a stalker? They'd laugh at her, possibly not to her face but definitely after she'd left. Where was the proof? There wasn't any.

She finished her breakfast, tidied up and gave herself a talking-to: forget about Tony. You might never hear from him again. She'd been brought up in a house where religion didn't play an important part but she prayed to God that she'd never have anything to do with Tony Goodson again.

'Good morning, everyone. Welcome to another week. I'm sorry you didn't get much of a break over the weekend but it'll all be worthwhile when these cases are solved.' Miles looked around the room to ensure everyone was present and paying attention.

'Any progress?'

'Boss, we've been checking Alessandra's bank accounts and social media,' said Tilly. 'Nothing exciting there. But we've found some interesting emails between Alessandra and Arthur Wilkinson. It seems he was quite sweet on her and wanted their relationship to go further. But she rebuffed him.'

'For those of you who don't know,' Miles interjected, 'Arthur Wilkinson is the managing director of the firm of solicitors Alessandra worked for. He's old enough to be her father – not that that should stop them having a romantic attachment. I think I need to have another word with him.'

James West jumped in: 'Boss, remember I told you about Kevin Dankworth, the guy who wasn't happy when he was sent down for grooming that young girl? He had a pretty rough time when he came out of prison, according to the probation service. They got him transferred to somewhere on the south coast where no one knew about his past and criminal record. He's trying to rebuild his life down there and I don't think he's come back to these parts to get revenge.'

West then told everyone about the BMW which was registered to a motor company on Lenton Lane.

'Obviously the killer's using false plates. But it's going to be difficult finding out where he got them from. There are numerous companies on the internet who'll knock you up some number plates and ask no questions.'

Miles looked at a file in front of him which contained a report from the pathologist.

'We've just heard that, like Daisy, Alessandra didn't have any water in her lungs and she was strangled before she went into the river. She was also sexually assaulted.

'We've had her car examined but the only DNA on it is Alessandra's.

'Next, and this could be vital: Alessandra had her phone with her when she was thrown into the canal. It stopped sending out a signal just after midnight. So we know that was the time of death. Let's check CCTV and ANPR cameras again to see if there were any other vehicles in the area around that time.

'We still haven't found Daisy's phone, so what does the fact that Alessandra had her mobile on her tell us about her killer? Is he getting careless? I don't think so. Like all psychopaths he's probably getting bored. That's why there are slight differences between the two killings.

'I think we can safely rule out that these two women were killed by a hitman. And I don't think they were victims of mistaken identity.

'Let's get the evidence to nail this guy, whoever he might be.'

46

On the second occasion Miles approached Arthur Wilkinson's house in Edwalton, he experienced a different ambience. He was no longer taken in by the splendour and size of the property; now he noticed lawns that hadn't been cut, flowerbeds that needed weeding and football goals that were rusting through being left outside in bad weather. Little work had been done in the autumn. Did this signify someone too busy to tend the garden or was it a sign of a lack of love in the house?

Wilkinson was wearing an unostentatious three-piece suit, white shirt and a sombre tie. He had bags under his eyes and there was a lot less colour in his face than Miles remembered.

'Thank you for delaying your journey to your office,' said Miles.

'No problem. Tea? Coffee?'

'No thanks. Now, Mr Wilkinson, I don't think you've been totally honest with us about your relationship with Alessandra.'

Wilkinson shuffled on his stool behind a breakfast bar. His leg twitched as he focused on what looked like a small patch of mud near the back door.

'I don't know what you mean.'

'Maybe I need to refresh your memory. We've been through Alessandra's emails and there are several from you which don't appear to have anything to do with your company's legal work. I wonder what your wife would say if she saw those emails?'

Wilkinson still didn't make eye contact.

'Inspector, my wife's no longer bothered about what I do or where I go. We've been married a long time. Too long, perhaps. We've seen our children grow up and move away. I suppose we just fell out of love. I think my wife and I merely papered over the cracks in our marriage for a long time for the sake of the children.

'Forty-five years is a long time, inspector. My firm's handled the divorces of people who were together for a much shorter time than that.'

Miles noticed resignation rather than remorse in Wilkinson's eyes.

'But you're still living under the same roof.'

'One of the benefits of having a large house. We live fairly separate lives.'

'And where's your wife now?'

'I've no idea. She has her own friends and spends a lot of time with them. Doesn't tell me when she's going out or when she's coming back. For all I know she could be cavorting with some toyboy at this very moment.'

'Anyway, these emails. You appear to be making certain suggestions to Ms de Villiers.'

'Nothing wrong with that. I took her under my wing when she joined the firm, watched her progress and we had a very good relationship.'

'But that wasn't enough for you, was it? You wanted to take that relationship further.'

Uncomfortable and nervous at the same time, Wilkinson took a while to reply.

'Inspector, my wife and I grew apart. But that doesn't mean I don't have feelings. I thought I could divert my emotions onto Alessandra. At first she was quite receptive. But then she pushed me away.'

'I remember you telling me she didn't mix work and pleasure,' said Miles. 'You must have been devastated when she rejected you.'

'Of course I was. But I'd never do anything to hurt her.'

'Mr Wilkinson, I think that you couldn't stand it when Alessandra told you, as she wrote in one email, to "act your age". You were distraught. Couldn't believe that she'd turn you down. Maybe you decided to get revenge. Perhaps

233

you couldn't face doing it yourself, so you got someone to do it for you. I'm sure you've come across enough people in your line of work who'd be willing to give you a hand. You'd quite easily be able to pay someone to do that, wouldn't you?'

Wilkinson jumped off his stool, his face flushed with rage.

'Inspector, I loved Alessandra far more than I ever loved my wife. I was hoping to get her to change her mind. I still thought we could have a future together. My kids would probably never speak to me again if we did strike up a relationship. After all, she was only a few years older than they are. But I didn't care. I just wanted us to be together.'

47

Cameron White eased his lithe but aching body into his seat on the Cape Air flight. A smile was fixed to his face despite his aching muscles: he'd had a productive tournament which had culminated in the team he was guesting for winning the final by a comfortable margin.

He was anticipating all the offers that would come his way when clubs from a wide range of countries contacted his agent about White's joining them for next season.

He'd not seen any of Syria: he'd heard it had a UNESCO world heritage site with a hippodrome that went back to the Roman era and he would have relished going on a private tour to see it. But playing basketball had taken up all his time; returning to a country that might come under attack from its neighbours or suffer a devastating earthquake just to see a tourist attraction wouldn't be on his priority list.

White had downloaded a travel guide from the website *Against the Compass* which had told him everything he wanted to know about travelling to and from Syria. He decided not to opt for a flight from Damascus to London because he knew it would take more than a day with a fourteen-hour stopover in Baghdad and a further wait in Istanbul.

Instead he'd gone to the Al Somaria taxi and bus station in Damascus and hung around waiting for other people who were hoping to make a similar journey over the border into Lebanon, in particular the capital Beirut. After only about fifteen minutes there were enough passengers to share a taxi, bringing the cost down to only twenty dollars each. He was thankful everyone had the correct visa and they didn't experience any problems when they went through several checkpoints.

White had arrived very early for his flight, hoping to save a few hundred dollars on the generous fee he'd been given for his travelling expenses. He'd charmed the young woman at the check-in desk, his handsome looks and chivalrous manner persuading her to let him have an aisle seat in the emergency exit row so that he could stretch his legs and be comfortable enough in economy rather than business class.

He'd arranged for someone from the Storm to pick him up at Heathrow and drive him back to Derby where he knew he'd be able to make his CV even more alluring to potential employers.

He was looking forward to getting back to the East Midlands. There was a good group of guys at the Storm, they all knew one another's strengths and weaknesses and he enjoyed hanging out with them. It was a pity, he reflected, that Daisy wouldn't be there to meet him as well. But she'd just been a welcome distraction from the pressures of playing basketball – not that getting paid for doing something he was good at carried much pressure.

He was glad he'd chosen to play this year in England. He'd hoped it would rekindle his interest in his chosen sport and he'd definitely got back his desire for winning. Derby had been great for him and he'd been great for Derby. But it was time to search for a bigger prize.

'Tilly, what can you tell us about Cameron White?'

'Well, boss, on the face of it he's a fine, upstanding young man. From Long Island in New York State. Went to a Catholic high school, then to St Francis. That's a college in Brooklyn. Motto: *My God My All.* Their basketball team is known as the Terriers. Play in Division I of the NCAA.'

She looked around, seeing more than a couple of bemused looks on her colleagues' faces.

'If you don't know your basketball, that's the top level of college sports in the States. St Francis have never got to the final of one of the end-of-season tournaments even though they've been trying for over 100 years.

'In football terms – or as Americans say soccer – they're a bit like Fulham: old, well-established but they've never won anything.'

She looked towards the back of the room at a detective she knew to be a Fulham fan and smiled. A peevish look greeted her.

'So, White graduated with a Bachelor of Arts in economics. Didn't think he was good enough to be a professional basketball player, so he began studying for a business qualification. Seems as though he got bored with that and decided that he wanted to play basketball after all.

'He contacted an English coach who lives in New York and organises tours to Europe. Anyone who thinks they've got a bit of talent can sign up with him, play a few games over there and see if anyone wants to offer them a contract.

'White impressed a few clubs who were keen on him. He chose to play in Derby.

'But here's the interesting thing: at one point the Storm thought he wouldn't be able to play for them – he struggled to get a work permit. It appeared the authorities delved into his background and discovered the FBI were running a check on him.'

'But how come he was able to join the tour to England?' an inquisitive officer wanted to know.

'Tourist visa. It's classed as a holiday but they're allowed to play a couple of games as there's no promise of a job.

'Anyway, his work permit must have been sorted because the next thing we know is White's on a plane and making his debut for the Storm in their first game of the season.'

Miles jumped up, galvanized by what he'd heard.

'Good job, Tilly. I've got a friend who works for the FBI and coincidentally he lives in New York. I'll give him a bell, see if he can find out what Mr White was up to.'

48

Austin R Hollis II refused to look up as he entered the Jacob
K Javits federal office building at Foley Square in the civic
center neighbourhood of New York. The exterior with its
grey and black panels along with the glass in an irregular
shape didn't inspire him with confidence or a willingness to
go to work. He regarded it as a missed opportunity by the
architects to build something unique that would stand out as
a model of ingenuity – not a bland monolith with little to
commend it.

Although it was one of the busiest convention centers
in the United States, Hollis had no desire to mingle with the
vast number of people who found their way to Foley Square
for everything from a motor show with almost one thousand
cars and trucks on display to a conference for the legalised
cannabis and hemp industry.

He jabbed a button to bring a lift to the ground floor
and waited with impatience for it. He wished he'd stopped
off at Starbucks for his usual Americano with two extra shots
of Espresso to get him fired up for the day ahead. But within
seconds he was able to start his upward journey.

The lift passed the Department of Homeland Security
and the US Citizenship and Immigration Services before

stopping on the twenty-third floor, the field office of the Federal Bureau of Investigation.

He sat behind his desk and was about to sift through a mound of paperwork which had grown considerably overnight when his phone rang. He was surprised to hear an English accent.

'Hi, Austin. How're you doing?'

'Miles, what's up? Haven't heard from you for a long time. Been meaning to call you but you know how it is – catching criminals ain't a part-time job.'

'I know exactly how you feel. How's your wife and kids?'

'They're great. Or at least they were the last time I saw them. I've got a couple of really big cases which are taking up all my time. Anyway, I presume you didn't call to make small talk.'

Miles and Austin had met two years previously when the FBI had sent their agent to England. They were keen to share practices about hostage negotiation and the two men instantly formed a bond. Miles was hoping he'd get a trip to New York to compare different crime-fighting methods, but financial restraints meant foreign exchange trips had been put on hold. He didn't think they'd be reinstated any time soon.

Miles told Austin about his interest in Cameron White. 'Can't say I've come across him – but I don't take as much interest in basketball as you do,' said the American.

Recalling the time they'd spent together in England, Miles knew Austin wasn't a sports fan and had declined the offer of watching a ball game. He preferred a trip to the theatre or a classical concert. He'd been captivated when Miles took him to Derby Museum and Art Gallery to see an exhibition of Joseph Wright paintings. Austin had drooled over A Philosopher Lecturing on the Orrery and Miles bought him a print of the masterpiece.

Austin thanked him and said it would take price of place in his office – alongside of course pictures of his wife and two children.

'Leave it with me, Miles. I'll find out about this guy and get back to you.'

Tony Goodson was in a fantastic mood. A group of Nottingham residents who lived in private rented accommodation had contacted the East Midlands Express with concerns about their landlords and he'd been singled out to help.

He'd organised a meeting, booked a room in a city centre hotel and wrote a piece for the paper inviting anyone who wasn't happy with the service provided by their landlord to go along.

More than fifty people crammed into the room and Goodson had to supress a smile. Look sympathetic, he told himself, so that they won't hold back. It would make another front-page splash.

Tenants of all ages attended, some ready to vent their anger on whoever might be willing to listen, others looking uncomfortable and wondering whether there was any point in showing up.

Goodson had taken the precaution of contacting Citizens Advice and a representative introduced only as Angela was there to let tenants know about their rights.

A succession of people were eager to share their experiences about the poor treatment they'd received from their landlord. A heavily tattooed man with an overhanging beer belly complained about an infestation of vermin. An elderly woman who struggled to keep her balance when she stood up said in a matter-of-fact voice that she'd gone to the meeting simply to keep warm because her central heating hadn't been working for months.

There were other gripes about smelly drains, leaking roofs and draughty windows that needed replacing.

Some people grumbled about landlords not carrying out repairs they'd promised to do, others claimed they were being discriminated against because of their race or sex and one young woman brought gasps from virtually everyone in the room when she maintained her 'pervy' landlord had entered her flat without her permission while she was out.

With each new revelation Goodson swelled up with pride although he was careful not to show his elation. He was looking forward to writing up what he considered a gripping human interest story: he had a soft spot for people's hardships.

Towards the end of the meeting he turned to Angela, a smartly dressed woman in her mid-forties who disclosed that her charity had received almost double the number of complaints about unacceptable living conditions than in the previous year.

She was clear in her instructions to those who weren't happy with their accommodation: 'You should speak to your landlord and ask him or her to sort out the problem. Take someone with you for support – but if you're not happy about face-to-face contact, put everything in an email.

'If you don't get any satisfaction you should make a formal complaint with photographs of any damage. Don't forget to include receipts if you've had to pay out for anything; for instance, if you had to go to the laundrette because your washing machine broke down. And if the problem's affected your health, include a note from your doctor.

'Most problems can be fixed this way – but as a last resort you could go to court. That could be expensive, so come and have a word with us before you do. We can let you know whether you can get legal advice or help with paying court fees.'

Goodson stood up and thanked Angela for attending and for her excellent advice.

'What I think you should do now is form a committee so that you can keep up the pressure on these private landlords. Don't let them get away with anything. You're paying out your hard-earned money in rent – make sure you're getting the best possible service.'

He was about to close the meeting when a voice chimed up: 'You don't care what happens to these people. You're only doing this so you can see your name on the front page of the paper again.'

Goodson looked around and saw a familiar face.

'Hi, Monica. Didn't realise you live in private accommodation.'

'I don't. I came along to make sure these people know what you're really like.

'I know this man,' she said as people in the room began to take notice. 'He's not bovvered about the problems wiv your flats. He'll tell you what you want to hear, put the story in the paper and you'll never see him again – unless your landlord frows you out onto the streets. He'll be back then, claiming to be your friend – only so that he can get another scoop.'

Goodson looked hurt, hoping the tenants weren't swayed by Monica Evans' comments.

'I can assure everyone that the East Midlands Express is a campaigning paper that cares about its readers. There's a Bill going through Parliament to clamp down on rogue landlords who are profiteering by renting out squalid accommodation. The Express is supporting this Bill and has written to the government outlining the problems faced by people in this part of the country. We believe everyone deserves a safe place to live that's appropriate for the twenty-first century.'

'Big words. You're full of hot air,' Monica shouted as she slammed the door shut behind her.

49

Miles was rushing around, trying to pull everything together for the next team briefing, when his phone rang.

'Afternoon, Austin. Or is it still morning where you are?'

'It's morning. And it's snowing. We've had a pretty bad storm overnight. But the city's still operating as normal. A few flakes in your country and everything stops, doesn't it?'

'Everything apart from the police,' Miles remarked. 'We have to find a way to keep going. Mind you, any semblance of bad weather tends to put criminals off. They stay indoors where it's warm. It's the best form of crime prevention I've ever come across.'

Austin laughed. 'The criminals over here are made of sterner stuff. The rain don't put them off none.'

'So, to what do I owe the pleasure?'

'Your man Cameron White. Not a major-league criminal by any means. In fact he appears quite clever.

'As you know, one of the things we investigate is health care fraud. Seems that White claimed he'd picked up a knee injury during a game. He produced a doctor's report which said he needed surgery. His insurance company paid out – but there's no evidence of White having that surgery.

'And we've not been able to trace the doctor. What do you say in your country? He's done a runner.

'It was taking so much time to investigate that we decided not to proceed. Didn't stand in the way of him getting his work permit. We thought that if he was out of the country he was unlikely to cause us any more problems.'

Miles had lost count of the number of times he'd driven along the twisty road that linked two of the main routes in and out of Derby. At one end of Markeaton Lane was Kedleston Road, the site of the University of Derby, while at the other was Ashbourne Road, leading to the market town which was known as the gateway to the Peak District.

On a couple of occasions Miles had taken Jordan to the Mundy Play Centre on Markeaton Park, one of the most popular attractions in the East Midlands, where his son enjoyed splashing in the paddling pool or driving one of the motorised cars which made him feel so grown-up.

Markeaton Lane was also known for being the site of the city's only crematorium. Miles had been to services both as a family member or friend as well as attending as a police officer on an active investigation.

He wondered how much longer the crematorium which was built in the 1950s could survive. Owned by the city council, the building was showing its age and facing competition from a private venue nine miles away.

Markeaton had had a bit of a facelift, with a paint job and new curtains. But the Trent Valley Crematorium in Aston-on-Trent could accommodate more than forty extra mourners. And when a prominent member of the community died, Trent Valley could have an extra two hundred people standing and watching the service on a giant plasma screen.

The coroner had released Daisy's body but he'd taken the precaution of getting a pathologist to conduct a second post-mortem examination. The findings would be revealed only if someone was charged at a later date and the accused's defence team took issue with the coroner's conclusion.

Miles was grateful that Christine hadn't asked him to do anything towards arranging Daisy's funeral. He felt Christine and her family should be the ones to decide the form of service and what should go into it. He had to admit he didn't even know whether Daisy was a Christian.

He thought back to services he'd sat through at Markeaton, some with a vicar droning on almost interminably – although the maximum time allowed for the whole event was forty-five minutes – while others turned into a beautiful, touching recap of a person's life.

Whenever he went to that crematorium he recalled a humanist funeral he'd attended, noting that the family of the deceased seemed to want to cover all bases: the coffin was taken into the chapel to a recording of Led Zeppelin's *Stairway to Heaven*.

Miles looked up and was relieved to see the celebrant was an old friend of his. He'd played basketball with Chris Webb in his younger days and Miles had been delighted when the 6ft 4in, jovial, caring young man had entered the ministry.

Miles knew it would be a respectful, poignant service, that Chris wouldn't preach to the mourners and everything would run smoothly. Miles knew Chris would be able to step in if Daisy's brother who lived in Australia and had come back to England for the funeral broke down while he was delivering the eulogy.

A slideshow of photographs of Daisy at various stages of her life was playing as the mourners entered. Each image showed Daisy with a beaming smile whether she was on her own, with Joey, her mother or a friend.

As her coffin was brought into the chapel to the tune of the Beatles' *Here Comes the Sun*, Miles looked around – and was disturbed to see Tony Goodson alone at the back.

What on earth did he want, Miles thought. Surely Goodson didn't think he would get anything from the grieving family on this of all days?

The emotional service included the Twenty-Third Psalm and a poem Joey had written about his mum which had a large number of people reaching for tissues.

After Miles had made his contribution to the collection – it was for a charity that provided support and stability to single mothers – he went outside to look at the lavish display of floral tributes.

'Good morning, detective inspector. Lovely service, wasn't it?'

Miles froze. He was about to lay into Goodson for his lack of sensitivity but stopped. Losing his temper would show a lack of respect for Daisy and would make the day worse for Christine.

'Yes. A really good send-off.'

'How's the investigation going – any comment?'

Miles moved in closer to Goodson and lowered his voice: 'I don't know why you're hanging around here. You weren't invited, but I suppose no one could stop you coming.

'Now, disappear so that these poor people can mourn in private. And if you want a comment from the police, go through the proper channels.'

50

'Miles, you won't believe it: we've got another body.'

He detected a note of resignation in the duty inspector's tone. Or was it inevitability?

'Nottingham canal. Woman in the water. We don't know yet if it's similar to Daisy Higgins and Alessandra de Villiers – but my money says it is. You could be dealing with a serial killer.'

That's all I need, Miles thought. 'Thanks. Let's hope that if it *is* another murder, and not a copycat killing, someone's left us with a few decent clues.'

Whenever anyone spoke about Nottingham canal, Miles recalled happy times on balmy summer evenings with a drink in his hand surrounded by people he enjoyed spending time with.

He could picture green and red narrowboats chugging at such a leisurely pace that anyone going along the towpath could walk faster without breaking into a sweat.

Miles had occasionally strolled along the path himself on a day off, enjoying the quiet surroundings – fishermen looking as though they didn't care if they got a bite, ducks and geese oblivious to anyone encroaching on their space –

before returning to the frenetic pace of the city centre which was merely a few hundred yards away.

But those memories were fading as Miles contemplated the discovery of what he assumed was another murder victim.

'Morning, boss.' Tilly's voice disturbed his thoughts but he considered it a welcome distraction.

His face lightened as he looked forward to another day working with the woman who he'd come to regard as indispensable.

'Hi, Tilly. I'd offer to get you a coffee but that'll have to wait.'

The A60 London Road had been cordoned off between the Boots Island and Meadow Lane, bringing that part of the city to a standstill.

Miles and Tilly met the crime scene manager who told them a shift worker walking to a nearby factory had spotted the body under a bridge. There was no one else in the area at the time. Uniformed officers would be questioning guests at a hotel at the bottom of the street. They'd also check for CCTV.

'What have you got?' Miles asked.

'Woman, probably middle to late fifties. Fingers cut off.'

'Sounds familiar. Any ID?'

'Yes.'

Miles was grateful that they wouldn't have to spend valuable time finding out who the latest victim was and could concentrate on uncovering evidence that the killer might have left.

'Her purse was in the inside pocket of her coat. Banker's card in it. The name on the card: Monica Evans.'

Tilly froze. 'Boss, I know that name.'

'Me too. She's the woman who used to be Ken Thompson's cleaner. Taking action against us for shooting him outside his house.'

'It look like the same *MO* as the two other deaths. But do you think she could have any links to Daisy and Alessandra?'

'Don't know. But one thing I'm certain about: we're dealing with a psychopath. And what's really concerning me is that the time between the murders is getting shorter.'

Whenever John Huntingdon used to visit a psychiatric hospital, he had a sense of the experience being surreal. He'd assessed scores of people during his career but the feeling never went away.

He thought he was going into a different world when he went through the gates of a secure hospital no matter whether it boasted the most up-to-date facilities or was built in Victorian times.

But that was before the Covid pandemic. Since then visits had been discouraged and he had to assess patients or prisoners via a video link. He didn't like it at all – how was he expected to tell if the person in front of him was settling into new surroundings whether that was a hospital or the remand wing of a prison?

Huntingdon made sure the camera and microphone on his computer were turned on before he made the conference call. A prison officer at the other end made the connection and Huntingdon saw Phillips in an interview room.

The forensic psychologist noticed a large inspection window in the door. The lighting was soft and there was nothing to use if patients thought about barricading themselves in the room. A chair chosen for its lightness rather than comfort and a spartan desk gave off an unwelcoming feel. To one side Huntingdon spotted the obligatory panic button which he hoped no one would have to use.

He took another brief look at Phillips' medical record that confirmed he'd been diagnosed with a dissociative disorder which meant he had at least two separate identities.

Huntingdon asked Phillips a series of questions about both his physical and mental health, discovering he hadn't been taking his medication. He put the blame for that on his mother who he claimed had failed to remind him when he should take it. When she died he forgot about it altogether.

After a while Phillips' mind began to wander and he appeared to lose concentration.

'Anything wrong?' asked Huntingdon.

Phillips muttered something about not staying there any longer. When Huntingdon pressed him, Phillips spoke incoherently, mentioning a meeting with the king and talking about the meat Phillips was providing for a banquet the monarch was attending.

From then on the interview deteriorated, with Phillips making a series of grunts. Huntingdon tried to question him about why he'd killed Felicity and cut up her body but Phillips became anxious and wouldn't answer.

Huntingdon was convinced he could make a case that Phillips didn't know what he was doing when he dismembered Felicity. His reliance on his mother gave him a distorted view of women, so much so that on her death he was unable to form any meaningful relationship. His personality disorder was heightened when Felicity rejected him by not responding to his email.

When Alessandra was murdered, Huntingdon felt he owed it to her to continue with the Phillips' assignment. He was determined that her final case would have the ending she wanted.

51

No matter how early Miles got to the office, the mountain of paperwork he had to sift through before he could convene the morning briefing seemed to get bigger every day.

He hadn't even had time to grab a coffee before all kinds of people in police HQ wanted his attention. And then his office phone rang. It was a voice that sounded vaguely familiar.

'Good morning, inspector. It's Simon Powell from the Express. How are you?'

'I'm okay, thanks. But I don't think there's anything I can help you with. I'm afraid I'll have to ask you to speak to the press office. That's where any updates will come from.'

Didn't take long for news of a third murder to get out, Miles thought.

'Hang on. That's not why I'm calling. I think I might have something that'll interest you.'

Miles had always respected Powell who he regarded as a good, sensible reporter who would never twist facts to make up a story. Miles was intrigued and gave the journalist his full attention.

'This is just between you and me, okay?'

'If that's what you want. No one else at your paper needs to know that you've made this call.'

'Thanks. I've been looking at the three murders you're investigating. Don't get me wrong – I'm not trying to tell you your job. But they've all got one thing in common.'

Miles had so far failed to find anything that linked the deaths. The women didn't know one another and came from different walks of life.

'On the night each woman was murdered, the Express's chief reporter, Tony Goodson, was covering a meeting quite near where the bodies were found.

'He wrote up the stories and they all appeared on the front page of the paper. The following day Goodson was . . . how shall I say . . . in an excited state. He didn't have to come into the newsroom; as you know, most of us work from home these days. But he was gloating. A couple of the guys in the newsroom thought it was because he was glad to have the top news story. But I'm not so sure.

'The guy's a narcissist. Always wants to be the centre of attention. It wouldn't surprise me to hear that he was involved in some way with these murders.'

Miles paused, his brain working overtime to try to make sense of what Powell had told him.

'You still there, inspector?'

'Sorry, Simon. Just thinking. I can see where you're coming from. I remember Goodson writing all three stories. But what connection did he have to the women? As far as we're concerned, he didn't know any of them.'

Powell couldn't disguise the disdain in his voice: 'I can't help you there. But did you know Monica Evans had a go at Goodson during that tenants' meeting? I think she saw through him and knew what he was like. I wouldn't put it past him to have stalked Monica after the meeting. The following day he came into the office with scratch marks on one side of his face. When I asked him what had happened, he said his cat had done it. But he hesitated before answering. I didn't believe him. Not one bit.'

Miles was intrigued. 'I want to know more about Goodson. What can you tell me about him?'

'He gives me the creeps. He makes out that he wants to pass on his experience to the younger members of the newsroom but he's just in it for himself.

'And he tries to make out he's related to the Curzons – you know, the family who live at Kedleston Hall. Says Curzon was his grandmother's maiden name. Reckons he should be living there. But I bet he's never done his family tree. He knows he'd find they're not his ancestors.

'And he can't take criticism. Someone tried to have a bit of a joke with him, said his grammar wasn't up to much in one of the stories he'd written. Reckoned a journalist of his calibre should have a better grasp of the English language. Goodson went berserk. Threatened to take the guy outside and show him some respect.'

Miles thanked Powell for the information. 'Oh, one other thing: where were you on the nights the three women were murdered? It's just routine, so that we can eliminate you from our enquiries.'

Powell was taken aback by the question but responded without hesitating: 'I'm on the sports team at the Express. It's been busy lately with our football teams involved in cup competitions. I was covering games on all three evenings.'

'And did you go straight home afterwards?'

'No. I went to the office to write up my piece for the next day's paper.'

'That's a bit unusual, isn't it? I thought reporters worked from home these days.'

'Most of us do – but we can still go into the office if we want to. I've got a good reason for doing that.'

'Go on,' urged Miles.

'I need somewhere quiet to write. Can't concentrate if it's too noisy. My wife's recently given birth to twins. She's up with them at all times of the night. I've tried writing my match report at home but it takes too long and I don't get enough sleep. It's better for everyone if I write in the office, get it done quickly and then go home.'

Miles suddenly remembered the time.

'Simon, thanks very much for this. Leave it with me. We'll have a look at Mr Goodson and see what we can come up with. And please – don't mention this to any of your colleagues for the time being. If there's anything in this you'll be the first to know.'

52

Miles assembled his team for another briefing and tried to get everyone focused. He noticed a sense of resignation in a couple of his officers who were frustrated at their lack of progress. He also detected a hint of boredom from two hard-working detectives who'd been given some of the more mundane tasks which had to be done with all investigations.

'Listen up. I've just had a report from Phillips' defence team. As you probably expected, they're going to claim that he wasn't responsible for his actions when he dismembered Felicity Strutt's body. They reckon he was suffering from something called DID. It's not something I'm familiar with.'

'That's dissociative identity disorder. Probably more common than you think.'

The room went silent as Paul Allen spoke. Not the person they knew as a perennial joker but someone with a greater knowledge than they expected.

'Dissociation: it's one way the brain copes with stress or trauma. It can be a short-term thing but it can also go on for a long time after someone's experienced a difficult situation.

'Dissociation may mean there are gaps in your memory when you can't remember particular events. You might go somewhere and forget how you got there.'

'I do that all the time when I'm driving. Especially when I'm on my way home from the pub! Does that mean there's something wrong with me?' a junior detective asked.

'No. There has to be other factors. You might think objects have changed shape or size. You feel like you're living in a dream or you're having an out-of-body experience; you're watching yourself from afar.'

One disbeliever cried out: 'Come off it – that only happens in the movies!'

Miles leaned against a desk and smiled. He had a new respect for Allen. 'Didn't know about your interest in cerebral matters.'

'It's just a hobby of mine. It can come in handy sometimes when I'm trying to get into the mind of a criminal.'

Miles looked around at impressed as well as shocked faces. He said: 'Philips has been examined and the defence will argue that Billy experienced changes in his identity. Reckon he had different personalities with different ages. Didn't remember what happened when another part of his identity was in control. He even spoke in different voices and used different names. The conclusion is that one of his other identities killed Felicity, not Billy himself.'

'Well, let's make sure we charge all his identities!' Allen joked.

His remark lightened the mood in the room. But Miles was concerned. Whatever happened, he believed Phillips would be detained for a long time. But would that be in prison or a psychiatric hospital?

Tony Goodson had a smug look on his face. Miles had never liked him and he had no desire to be in a small interview room sitting opposite him. But he realised he had to maintain as professional an attitude as possible while they were in each other's presence.

'Thanks for coming in, Mr Goodson. Or can I call you Tony?'

Goodson waved a hand and shrugged. 'Tony's fine.'

'This is my colleague, Detective Sergeant James West. You're here to help us with our enquiries into the deaths of three people, Daisy Higgins, Alessandra de Villiers and Monica Evans.

'I'd like to point out that you're here voluntarily to make a witness statement and you're free to leave at any time.'

'Naturally I want to do everything I can to help. We all want to find out who murdered those poor, desperate women who were unable to defend themselves. Tragic cases.'

Miles nodded without revealing how sanctimonious he thought Goodson was.

'Now, Tony, you seem to have been busy recently. Your name's been on the front page on a number of occasions.'

'I can't help it if I'm an excellent reporter. I tend to have a knack of being able to sniff out a good story.'

And I have a knack of smelling bullshit, Miles thought.

'You've had several articles that have made the headlines. Can we go through them? The day after Daisy died you wrote a story about a meeting in Sudbury. Local people were concerned at the number of inmates absconding from the open prison. Daisy was at that meeting.

'Then you had – what's it called? – a front-page splash about knife crime. Bereaved relatives were calling for the police to do more. Alessandra was at that meeting.

'And finally the story of tenants complaining about private landlords. Living in squalor, I think you described it. Monica attended that meeting.

'It seems odd to us that these murders occurred the day before your coverage in the East Midlands Express. Would you like to say anything about that?'

Goodson hesitated for a couple of seconds longer than Miles expected.

'Inspector, every time there's a death that's out of the ordinary my boss puts me onto it. He knows I'm the best man for the job. If there's a story to be uncovered, I'll uncover it.'

'But three murders, one after the other?'

'Coincidence. And remember this, inspector: I've had loads of stories about corrupt councillors, celebrities who've crossed the line with their sexual behaviour and businessmen who've been involved in dodgy deals. And nothing happened to any of *them.*'

Miles was quick to respond: 'So, for the record, what were your movements on those evenings after the meetings?'

'Isn't it obvious?' Goodson said with a sneer. 'I went back to the office to write up my copy for the next day's edition. I like to give the sub-editors plenty of time to make my story the best. It'd be there as soon as they logged on the next morning.'

'And was there anyone else in the building who can corroborate that?'

'Inspector, you only get where I am by working harder than all your colleagues. No one else was working that late – they were all safely tucked up at home in their beds.'

53

'Okay, what have we found out about Daisy Higgins?' Miles asked.

Tilly addressed the room with the confidence and poise that came from working closely with uniformed officers who'd been looking into Daisy's background.

'We've spoken to people who lived near her. She's kind, helps others whenever she can. There's an elderly woman a couple of doors away; Daisy used to do some shopping for her, went to the supermarket a couple of times a week, made sure she had everything she needed.

'The mothers at her son's school all got on well with her. She'd always offer to take someone else's child to football training or swimming. If anyone was struggling to pick their child up afterwards, Daisy would make sure they got home safely. The only time she couldn't do anything was when there was a clash with a Derby Storm game.'

Tilly waited while her tablet PC loaded up the next page of her notes.

'It's a similar picture at the basketball club. She was a highly regarded employee. She was great at her job and she loved it. Last season she was nominated for executive of the year. She missed out because it was awarded to someone who was rumoured to be a distant relative of the league's chairman.

'When I asked her colleagues what her reaction was when she didn't get the award, they said she wasn't bothered in the slightest – she got job satisfaction and that was all she wanted.'

Miles weighed up everything he heard.

'That confirms what I knew about Daisy and adds a bit more. But it doesn't tell us who would want to kill her or why.

'Let's look at possible scenarios. Daisy didn't have a criminal record. Not even a parking ticket. She'd joined an anti-drugs group at the local senior school. Even got some of the Storm players to talk to the kids and warn them of the dangers. So at this stage we can rule out anything to do with drugs.

'Jealous lover or ex-partner?. Unlikely. From what I know Daisy wasn't in a relationship and hadn't been for some time.

'Where does that leave us? Disgruntled person who used to work at the Storm? Anything on that, Tilly?'

'Possibly. Daisy was well liked, we know that. But from what I've picked up she had a steely side too. She helped to negotiate players' contracts. Made sure they weren't too big for their boots, if you'll excuse the pun. But what if there was someone who felt he was worth a huge salary, the sort of money NBA players or Premier League footballers get? He might have thought he wasn't getting what he was worth and took his anger out on Daisy.'

Miles thought immediately about Yandel Eliot. The previous season the 6ft 10in (2.08m) centre had been a huge favourite at the Storm: he was mobile for a big man, was strong under the basket and had a few flashy moves that brought the crowd to their feet. But Miles recalled there was something that didn't feel right about Eliot.

'Tilly, wasn't Yandel Eliot implicated in a drugs problem before he came to England?'

'Yes, boss. I remember speaking to his old coach. Said drugs were found in the accommodation Eliot shared with a student when they were at college. Eliot denied having anything to do with the drugs but he was suspended from the basketball team. Disappeared for a while before he showed up again in Derby.'

'He was quite good at disappearing,' Miles contributed. 'If I remember correctly he packed his bags and cleared off before the end of the season. Left the Storm in a bit of a mess.

'Try and find him, Tilly. Maybe he decided to sneak back into this country and settle a few scores.

'But that's not the only thing we should be concentrating on. Who was the last person to see Daisy on the night she was murdered? She went to that meeting about Sudbury open prison. I want to know who else was there, who she spoke to and if she left with anyone. We haven't found her phone, so that meeting is the best chance we've got of piecing together her last movements.

'I've got the pathologist's report on Monica Evans. No water in her lungs. Strangled. Sexually assaulted.

'We need to know more about who Monica associated with. Let's go.'

54

'This is becoming a habit!' Tilly laughed as she and Miles revelled in another Storm victory.

Cameron White was outstanding as Derby routed Caledonia Gladiators 113-84 – not a simple task as Scotland's leading club were always reluctant to surrender to any team from south of the border. But White was unstoppable, shooting over smaller guards when they tried to mark him and exploding to the basket every time Caledonia put a bigger defender on him.

As the two detectives headed to the bar they heard a familiar voice: 'good to see you can take time off from catching criminals to come and watch a game.'

Miles offered an outstretched hand to Marcus Carter, the Storm's ebullient owner who until recently had been a bit of an enigma. All people knew about him was that he was a successful businessman who'd been interested in basketball and seized the opportunity to bring the sport back to the city.

He usually shunned publicity but on the first anniversary of his taking over the club he allowed the East Midlands Express to write a story about him. He revealed he had a passion for basketball which could be used to build a 'family' that had a prominent position in the community.

The writer of the article was able to quote part of Carter's background including that he was born and raised in Derby and made his money through spotting a gap in the wellbeing market. He tapped into a trend of people being concerned about improving their life expectancy, came up with an app which gave all sorts of health and exercise tips – and then sold it for several million pounds.

'We try not to miss a home game – you're guaranteed a good night's entertainment. And it's still pretty cheap,' Miles beamed.

Carter leaned in so that no one else could hear: 'Keep this between ourselves, but if we keep winning we could be playing in Europe next season.'

Miles took advantage of Carter's good mood to ask a favour.

'I've got a group of kids over in Nottingham who are getting up to mischief. They're bored. They want something to occupy them. They're into basketball but they've got nowhere to play.'

The smile vanished from Carter's face.

'Nottingham? That's the dark side! Have you forgotten the animosity that Derby and Nottingham have for each other? You want *me* to do something for those kids at the other end of the A52?'

His eyes lit up again. 'I'm joking. Anything you want. If they're basketball fans they're okay by me.'

'Any chance I could bring them over here to play?' Miles asked.

'We're pretty full up most of the time but I think we can squeeze them in. Who are you going to get them to play against?'

'Well, I wouldn't want them to play one of your teams – I don't want to put them off and see them get hammered in their first game. I'll get together a team of coppers. They won't be all that good – and I'm sure the Nottingham lads will revel in the chance to get a bit physical against us.'

Carter realised that there might be benefits for the Storm.

'Tell you what: I'll get one of the academy coaches to referee the game. Then if any of your lads impress us, we'll give them a trial.

'And I don't suppose any of them have got transport. I'll have a word with the company we use to take our teams and supporters to away games. We'll sort out a minibus to bring them over from Nottingham and take them back again.'

'That's fantastic. Thanks very much,' said Miles who hoped this would get the Chief Constable off his back.

Suddenly he remembered what he'd been meaning to ask Carter.

'By the way, did you ever hear anything about Yandel Eliot and where he is now?'

'Don't mention him! One of the worst signings we ever made. Not the right attitude to be a member of the Storm family at all. Couldn't care less about what happened to him. But I did hear one of the Caledonia players say they'd heard he'd gone to South America.'

Simon Powell answered his phone and was surprised to hear Miles' voice.

'Hello, inspector. Anything to report?'

'Morning, Simon. You may not be able to answer this question because you don't go into the Express office very often. But do you know when the cleaners are in?'

'As a matter of fact I do. There's only one cleaner. You know, cutbacks. The Express used to contract the work out to a big cleaning firm but then the management decided they couldn't afford it. Now it's a lovely lady called Pat who comes in quite late in the evenings. Cleans a couple of other offices first. Takes her longer than it ought to because she'll stop and have a chat with anyone who's in. Sometimes makes a cup of tea as well.'

'So she might know whether Tony Goodson was in the office writing up his stories on the nights the three women were killed.'

'Her memory might not be that good. But I can tell you categorically that he wasn't in on any of those nights.'

Miles perked up, desperate to hear Powell's thoughts.

'Go on.'

'Didn't I tell you? The murders coincided with football matches I was covering. I went back to the office to write up my reports. Goodson wasn't there at all. On any of those evenings.'

55

Tony Goodson shuffled in the uncomfortable seat. He had no desire to be in this claustrophobic, unwelcoming room for a second time, but DI Davies had been insistent that he should turn up for another 'chat', as he put it.

Goodson didn't want to talk to anyone at the moment, least of all an officious policeman who was struggling to make any progress in the three murders he was investigating.

'Is this going to take long? You do know I've got a deadline to meet?'

Miles disliked Goodson even more than on the previous occasion they'd met. But he kept his emotions under control and retained a professional aura. James West said nothing.

'Mr Goodson – '

'Tony. You can call me Tony.'

'Mr Goodson. You've not been totally honest with us, have you?'

'Inspector, you know what a bad reputation journalists have. Caused of course by some scurrilous national reporters. I think the only way for the public to take us seriously is for us to tell the truth at all times.'

'Admirable sentiment, Mr Goodson. It's a pity you don't practise what you preach.'

Goodson stayed as still as possible. He imagined Davies had studied body language and didn't want to give anything away with his movements.

'I'm afraid I don't know what you mean.'

'You told us that on the nights when Daisy Higgins, Alessandra de Villiers and Monica Evans were murdered, you went to the offices of the East Midlands Express to file your story. But we've heard from one of your colleagues who was working late on each of those evenings. They reckon you never showed up. Not once.'

'Who told you that?' Goodson blurted out.

'Never mind who. Is that correct?'

'Of course it's not. I was there and don't let anybody tell you otherwise. I bet it was one of the younger reporters. Wants my job. Do anything to get rid of me. Well, you can tell him this, inspector: I'm going nowhere. I'm irreplaceable.'

'How do you know it was a "he"?'

Goodson simply stared at Davies and West, revealing nothing.

'Thank you for coming in, Mr Goodson. I'll show you out.'

Goodson stomped his way back to reception, calling out to the two detectives as he made for the car park: 'I hope you realise I'm late with my story for tomorrow's edition. I've never missed a deadline – if I miss this one you'll be sure to hear from my editor.'

When he was out of earshot West uttered the question he'd been dying to ask.

'Boss, why didn't you arrest him? He's the one consistent factor when those three women were murdered. He's clearly the prime suspect.'

'Calm down, James. As Goodson said, he's going nowhere. We need more evidence before we can tie him to the killings. And I know how we can get it.'

Miles' enthusiasm was back to maximum as he welcomed his team to the next briefing.

'By now I think we've all come to the conclusion that a psychopath was responsible for all three murders. But I don't need to emphasise to you that we've still got to follow all lines of enquiry and be absolutely certain of someone's guilt before we arrest them.

'Any developments on Daisy Higgins?'

Tilly jumped in: 'I've found out where Yandel Eliot's playing: Argentina. He's been there since the start of the season. Hasn't missed a game. I spoke to someone at his new club who said he'd turned over a new leaf – hasn't missed a day's training. So he wouldn't have had time to get back to England and harm Daisy.'

Miles recalled a player who'd left Derby because he wanted to make big money in Argentina. His old Derby coach got a telephone call in the middle of the night asking for help to get him out of the country because someone had pulled a gun on him. Good luck to Eliot out there, Miles thought.

James West was next: 'Kevin Dankworth, the guy who threatened Alessandra, the barrister, the judge and anyone else who was responsible for sending him down. Moved to Brighton, changed his name and tried to start a new life. But the vigilante group that outed him – they got in touch with a similar organisation on the south coast. Made his life hell. He took his own life at the beginning of the year. Another one out of the frame.'

'Thanks, James. Now, what have we got on Monica Evans?' He didn't want to make assumptions but he expected that she wouldn't have had a lot in common with the other two victims.

'Boss, I've been looking into her background,' said Paul Allen.

'Good to have you back, Paul. Teeth okay now?'

'Yes, thanks, boss. I've had the wisdom teeth out but I've still got my brain. And my good looks.

'Anyway, Monica Evans: salt of the earth. Married when she was eighteen but separated several years ago. Didn't bother to get divorced. Three sons, all grown-up.

'She had casual jobs, serving in a café, cleaning – that's how she came to work for Ken Thompson. But she didn't have a criminal record and I don't think she fully understood what Thompson was up to.

'A few of her neighbours said she didn't take any nonsense from anyone – but she'd treat you right if you were okay with her.'

'Good job, Paul.

'Now, this could be good news. You know we've been unable to locate Daisy and Alessandra's mobile phones – but we've got Monica's. It's being examined to see what information we can get from it.

'So, what does this tell us? Is the killer becoming too cocky? Or was he disturbed and didn't have time to remove the evidence? Let's go through the witness statements again just to make sure we're not missing anything.'

Miles then adopted a stern look as he brought up a picture on one of the screens behind him.

'This is Tony Goodson. Chief reporter with the Express. He reported on a meeting each of the three women went to on the night they were murdered. He reckons he went back to the newspaper's office after those meetings. But another journalist maintains he and the cleaner were the only people in the building.

'One of them isn't telling the truth. I know who my money would be on. But we need evidence.

'I want CCTV from any building on the same street as the Express office, and I want it from 9pm until the early hours on the three evenings in question. If Goodson was there, we should have footage of him arriving at or leaving the office.

'Tilly, you're with me. We're going to have a word with the cleaner.'

56

Tilly took the wheel and drove to the east of the city to the St Ann's district. Her knowledge of Nottingham was improving although she still felt a relative newcomer. Her research had discovered that the area was named after St Ann, the patron saint of lacemakers and women who had difficulty conceiving.

The Victorian streets were replaced in the 1970s with what was known as a Radburn-style estate. Backyards of the houses faced the street while the fronts were opposite one another. A maze of walkways meant outsiders found huge difficulty getting where they wanted to go. Tilly found herself offering a prayer of thanks for the car's satnav.

The outside of Pat the cleaner's house was no different to any other in the neighbourhood. The inside was spotlessly clean despite innumerable knick-knacks and tat covering every surface.

Miles refused the offer of tea and hoped he didn't appear too eager to get the interview finished so that he could head back to HQ.

'Lovely place you've got here. Reminds me of my gran's,' Tilly said and saw a satisfied smile on Pat's face.

'Have you lived here long?'

'We moved here a few years after we got married.'

Miles' face remained impassive. He thought they were in for a long afternoon – but he knew that Tilly was getting on Pat's wavelength and she had a better chance of getting information out of her.

'Keith and I were together for forty-five years. I lost him last Christmas. Pancreatic cancer. He went really quick. He left me enough money to have a decent life, but I prefer to do a bit of work. Keeps me active. Gets me out of the house.'

'I bet you come across some awkward people as well as some nice ones.'

'Too right,' Pat told Tilly. 'I remember a couple of years ago I cleaned some offices in the centre. A big accountants' place. They were horrible. Treated me like dirt. Just because they made a lot of money and drove fast cars, they thought they could behave exactly how they wanted. When I left I told them it'd be a cold day before I went to work for them again.'

'Good for you!' Tilly tapped Pat's arm and grinned.

'You also clean at the Express, the newspaper, don't you?'

'Yes, I do. I couldn't expect a better welcome when I go there. I know journalists aren't everybody's cup of tea but they're all right with me. Mind you, since the pandemic there hasn't been as many people in the office.'

'And you go in the evenings, don't you?'

'Yes. There's a good bus service from here. Takes only five or six minutes to get to the city centre. The people at the Express asked me if I'd mind changing my hours. They said it'd be better at night when the building was almost completely empty. They wouldn't have done it if I objected. But because it didn't bother me, they gave me a pay rise.'

Tilly paused before her next question.

'Have you come across a man called Tony Goodson at the Express?'

Pat grunted. 'Huh. Him! Too big for his boots, that one.'

'How do you mean?'

'Well, when I used to clean during the day, he expected me to be at his beck and call. "Get me a cup of tea – two sugars. Take this to the boss. Go and get me a sandwich." I didn't like him at all. I don't think many of the other people working there did. Awful man. Oh, God forgive me – I shouldn't pass judgement.'

Miles was about to join the conversation but he could see that Tilly had built up a rapport with Pat.

'Did you see Mr Goodson after you changed your hours?'

'No, that was one of the good things about it. I never had to put up with him again.'

'What about Simon Powell?'

Pat didn't hesitate: 'Lovely lad. Tells me all about his wife and family. They've just had twins – did you know?'

'Yes,' Tilly said. 'Quite young, aren't they?'

'Simon's invited me to go round to their house and meet them. I can hardly wait.'

'Now, Pat, this is really important: have you seen Mr Goodson in the office at all, any night, say, in the past few weeks?'

'No.'

'Are you sure about that?'

'Course I am. Haven't seen him for months. Wouldn't bother me if I never saw him again.'

57

'Before we go any further, let's examine whether the evidence we've got so far points to a psychopath who carried out these murders.'

Miles took a long swig of coffee which was helping to keep him alert as the investigations were going on longer than he'd hoped.

'The so-called experts don't always agree on what constitutes a serial killer. They seem to change their minds depending on who's backing their research or who's putting up the money for their latest study.

'From what we know of our murderer, I'd categorise him as an organised killer.'

The team were all concentrating as much as possible, hanging on to every word Miles spoke.

'This type of killer is reckoned to be the most difficult to capture and convict. Likely to have a high IQ. Each phase is planned meticulously. Usually the organised killer won't leave any evidence. Our guy has left the odd clue – but I don't think that's down to a lack of planning: I think he's sending a message that he's better than us.'

Accessing the next page of his notes, he continued: 'Some serial killers need a reminder between murders of how they're in control, how much power they have. That's why they'll take a trophy. This could be a piece of jewellery, an item of clothing – or in our killer's case, his victims' fingers. He might be looking at them this very moment, planning his next attack.'

'What about the victims' mobile phones?' an experienced detective wanted to know.

'I have to admit I'm not sure. They could be trophies as well. They could also be his way of keeping us off the scent. He probably thinks that when mobile phones go under water, there's no chance of recovering information from them. But the tech boys can do all sorts of things these days. Let's hope they can get something from Monica's phone.

'The only thing we can be sure of is that our killer won't be able to empathise with his victims' pain – he'll just get pleasure from seeing them suffer. He exerts control over them in every possible way.'

News of the basketball game Miles was arranging for inner-city kids soon spread around police HQ. Everyone agreed that Miles was doing an admirable job – even the Chief Constable.

Miles was sent a congratulatory note from the big boss. He was astounded to see the suggestion at the end:

'You will of course let these young lads win the match, won't you, Miles?'

He was fuming. What did the Chief Constable know about basketball? Taking part was more important than winning, he understood that. But try telling that to some of his team mates who were so competitive they wouldn't let their three-year-old come out on top when they were playing the card game Snap. He just hoped the kids would be good losers – if they lost.

The minibus pulled into the car park at the Cloud Centre, leaving the young players a short walk as drizzle began to fall. 'Wow, look at this!' cried one. 'We're actually going to be playing here?' said another.

The police team consisted of a couple of guys who'd played at local league level, a few officers who'd hardly ever picked up a basketball, Miles, Tilly and another female detective. They welcomed the newcomers and directed them to their changing room.

Twenty minutes later the two teams had warmed up and the game began. On the first offence the police team turned the ball over when Miles passed to one of his team mates but he was looking in the opposite direction. The Nottingham lads raced up the court and laid the ball in for the first points of the game.

That sparked a ten-point run which forced Miles to call a time-out. It gave the police a welcome breather as well as allowing Miles to issue new instructions.

On the next police offence one of the visitors tripped Tilly as she was driving to the basket – but she managed to throw up a wild shot which somehow went through the hoop. Miles was about to warn the defender to take it easy – but Tilly waved him away, made the bonus shot awarded for the foul and gave him a wry smile.

The next time the police were in possession, Tilly set a solid screen which prevented the player who'd tripped her getting close enough to steal the ball. She rolled to the basket, took a well-measured pass and scored with a simple lay-up.

The game was physical, scrappy and exhausting. Miles found that the shooting touch which had been a feature of his game in his younger days hadn't left him and he scored a few baskets that kept the police team in contention. But the Nottingham lads proved to be fitter and faster in the fourth quarter, taking the game by fifteen points.

'Thanks, man. That was awesome,' the Nottingham captain told Miles. 'We're so grateful that you organised this. And what a court! Most of us could only dream of playing somewhere like this.'

'Glad you enjoyed it. Hope you see us in a different light now. We're not just about turning up when something bad's happened and arresting you for the sake of it.'

The captain held out his hand: 'Some of my guys never used to have a good word to say about the police. They'd been stopped and searched when they'd done nothing wrong. Weren't doing drugs or carrying a knife or anything.

'They've got a different opinion now. They realise you're just human beings doing your job. And anyone who likes basketball is good by us.'

58

'Hi, Miles. Come on up. I've got something for you.'

The digital forensics manager and Miles had an understanding. A call like this was usually good news.

Miles took the stairs two at a time and was only slightly breathless when he arrived.

The digital forensics manager was in his fifties, with greying, wavy hair swept back off his forehead and covering his collar in a style which some people thought would look better on a man a couple of decades younger. He wore a striped shirt, classy-looking jeans and new, white trainers. His glasses were attached to a chain around his neck; he felt it gave him a sophisticated air although his colleagues weren't so complimentary.

'Miles, we've been examining Monica Evans' phone. It's a long time since I've seen one as old as that. Didn't think you could still get them. It could be in a museum in a few years' time. But I suppose if all you want to do is make calls and send the odd text, it's good enough.

'I find putting a phone in a bag of cat litter gives better results than uncooked rice. Amazing what you can get once they've dried out.'

Miles was beginning to get exasperated but tried not to let it show.

'And what does the data tell us?'

'There's one number which crops up a fair bit. Monica and this person spoke several times in the past month. Obviously we've got no idea what the conversations were about. But Monica called this number a couple of hours before she died. This might be the last person she spoke to. Apart from her killer, of course.'

Miles rushed downstairs, almost falling over in his haste to get back to his office.

He sat down, removed a sheet of paper from the file the digital forensics manager had given him and called the last number on the list. A woman's voice answered.

Miles introduced himself and asked the woman's name. Helen Loudon sounded nervous, distressed even. He explained he was investigating Monica Evans' death and Helen could have been the last person to speak to her on the night she died.

'Monica called me to give her apologies. We were supposed to meet up but she cancelled. Said there was an important meeting she had to go to.'

'And how did you react?'

'I was disappointed but that was all. She said she'd call me the next day to sort out another time to catch up. But she never rang. Then I heard that she'd been murdered. I still can't believe it.'

Miles wanted to know more about the two women's relationship.

'We met a few months ago. At a grief counselling session. I lost my young son; Monica was grieving for her boss. He was shot by the police.'

The details came flooding back to Miles, in particular the headlines in the East Midlands Express.

'Do you know a guy called Tony Goodson?'

'Yes. He interviewed me after Jack's death. Wanted me to sue the health authority. At first I thought he was a really nice man. Then I realised he was only in it for himself. Monica convinced me to have nothing to do with him. I'm really going to miss her.'

Miles became concerned: 'Are you alone at home?'

'Yes. Why?'

'Lock your door and don't let anyone in unless it's the police.'

Ten minutes later Miles and James West were speeding towards Helen's house, lights blazing and sirens blaring. The adrenalin was pumping through his body and his stress levels were high. He calmed down when he arrived at Helen's address and saw her watching through the lounge window. He showed his warrant card and she let them in.

'What's this all about, inspector?'

'I don't want to alarm you but you could be in danger.'

He told her that Goodson was a prime suspect in the murder of her friend Monica.

'What we can do is offer you protection. Keep you somewhere safe until all this blows over. There's no guarantee the killer won't strike again. What do you say?'

Helen was stunned. Was this really happening?

'How long will it be for?'

'We can't say. Just until we've got someone in custody.'

Helen asked another question although it pained her to do so: 'What if it isn't Goodson? What if he's innocent?'

'Well, that'll mean we'll have to look after you a little bit longer.'

'Inspector, I've had enough upheaval recently to last me a lifetime. What if I say no?'

Miles had anticipated her answer.

'We'll get officers on patrol to pop by on a regular basis. But it won't be as secure as having you in a safe house where no one will be able to get to you.'

Helen answered a little too quickly for Miles' liking.

'I'll take my chances here. I'd be bored anywhere else. I need familiar things around me. I'm still trying to adjust after losing my son.

'I stood Tony Goodson up a couple of weeks ago. He was angry. Really angry. But if he wanted revenge he'd have got it by now.'

Miles showed himself out and thought: I hope you're right.

59

The CCTV analyst called Tilly over to show the young detective what the team had discovered by searching through hundreds of hours' footage from the streets around the East Midlands Express office.

'Here we have pictures from a building just across the road from the Express. It's good quality – no need to enhance it. We've not found anyone matching Goodson's description going into the Express on the nights when the three women were murdered.

'Now, look at this. A bit later on, on each occasion, we've got someone coming *out* of the office. You showed me the photo of Simon Powell – that looks like him. He was telling the truth.'

And Goodson wasn't, Tilly concluded.

Seconds later Miles and James West returned from their visit to see Helen Loudon. 'Boss, we've got him!' Tilly enthused.

'Okay, but let's play this by the book. James, take Paul with you. Check whether Goodson's at his home address. In the meantime I'll liaise with the tactical firearms commander and he can get authorisation for a firearms team. We'll make sure they've got all resources available – dogs, helicopter, the lot. We need to be fully prepared for any eventuality.'

Several hours later, with everyone in place, the tactical firearms commander gave the word for the door of Goodson's house to be forced open. The sound of a wooden door splintering was the start of a cacophony of noise, with shouts of 'Armed police!' and 'Stay where you are and no one will get hurt!' It was followed by heavy footsteps as officers thudded upstairs or burst into rooms to check for occupants.

A startled Goodson was brought out, his hands secured behind his back, after being formally arrested. Maintaining his innocence, he threatened to invoke the full might of the national press, the Prime Minister and the Independent Office of Police Complaints on Miles' team for wrongful arrest.

Miles thanked the tactical firearms commander that everything had gone smoothly.

'Not sure about that. There was a terrible smell when we went in. Found an old lady motionless in a chair. We've called an ambulance.'

After Goodson had been booked into the custody suite he insisted on having his lawyer present when he was interviewed. A solicitor from one of the most expensive, prestigious practices in Nottingham, if not the Midlands, appeared, his Savile Row suit only one of the trappings paid for by his company's exorbitant fees.

'Now, Tony,' he began.

'Mr Goodson to you.'

He was taken aback but pressed on.

'Mr Goodson. These are very serious charges and my advice to you is that you should reply "no comment" to every question the police put to you until we know what evidence they've got.'

'Don't tell me what to do. I'll answer whatever I want. You're there to make sure they don't overstep the mark legally.'

This should be an interesting session, the solicitor thought.

The two of them were led into an interview room where Miles and James West joined them moments later.

'Mr Goodson, may I remind you that you are under caution. I don't believe you were honest with us before. You told us you were in the offices of the East Midlands Express on the nights when Daisy Higgins, Alessandra de Villiers and Monica Evans were killed. Do you recall saying that?'

'Yes, I do,' said Goodson, his solicitor watching him closely.

'We don't believe you were at the Express when you said.'

'I told you before – someone's after my job. They're jealous of my success.'

'We've got witnesses who'll testify that you didn't go into the office on those dates. And we have CCTV footage which tells a similar story.'

Any optimism the solicitor had that the police didn't have a particularly strong case evaporated. 'I'm advising my client to make no further comment,' he interjected.

'Shut up! I'll say what I like.'

Miles recognised that Goodson was aiming to control the interview – one of the dominant signs of a psychopath.

'There must have been something wrong with those cameras. You can doctor CCTV so that it gives a completely false picture.'

Miles adopted a harsher tone: 'Did you murder Daisy Higgins?'

'No.'

'Did you murder Alessandra de Villiers?'

'No.'

'Did you murder Monica Evans?'

'No. I certainly did not.'

'You've been told about the unfortunate death of your mother. Sorry for your loss. Did you kill her?'

'Of course I didn't.'

'Then why didn't you get medical help for her? Wasn't it clear from the smell in your house that she'd passed away?'

'I have a problem with my nose. No sense of smell.'

'Thank you, Mr Goodson. That's all for now.'

'Am I free to go?'

'I'm afraid not. We'll resume this interview later. In the meantime, you'll be taken back to your cell.'

Miles had never found it harder to suppress a smile.

60

The woman leading the CSI team who'd taken Goodson's house apart presented the initial findings to Miles.

In a basement which had been secured with a double lock they found three jars with fingers preserved in the embalming agent formaldehyde. A number of empty jars were sitting on a lower shelf. The team also recovered two mobile phones which were thought to belong to Daisy and Alessandra; dark clothing which they sent off for analysis; and a pair of false number plates. Miles was sure these would match the ones captured on camera near the murder scenes.

Goodson's mobile phone and laptop were bagged up, with instructions that they should be examined at the earliest opportunity.

Eventually Miles got the results he'd been expecting: the fingers did belong to Goodson's three victims, their DNA was found on his clothes and it was confirmed that the two recovered phones belonged to Daisy and Alessandra.

Goodson's phone was even more revealing: on the night of the murders it hadn't left Goodson's house; another ploy to convince police that he was nowhere near the scene of the killings.

Miles was ready for another bout of questioning with Goodson.

West started the recording equipment and everyone introduced themselves. Before they could go any further, Goodson's solicitor said he wanted to read out a statement.

'This is a statement signed by Anthony Wilfred Goodson. I should like to state that I had absolutely nothing to do with the three murders for which I have been charged. I confirm that I have only a passing acquaintance with one of the women who died. I should also like to state that I do not have any inkling as to who might have killed them. I should like to stress that I am innocent of all the charges. In view of this, I shall be making "no comment" to any questions put to me in this interview.'

Miles knew he still had to put those questions to Goodson even if he got the same unresponsive answer to each one. But he felt Goodson would want to be in control and would incriminate himself when Miles revealed more evidence.

'Mr Goodson: thank you for your statement. I'm quite prepared to accept that you didn't know Daisy Higgins or Alessandra de Villiers. But you knew Monica Evans, didn't you?'

'No comment.'

Miles opened his tablet PC at a front-page story on the East Midlands Express. The headline read: **Crime boss: 'traumatised' worker to sue police.**

'Do you remember that story? It's got your byline on it.'

'No comment.'

'I don't think you could have got that story without having a good relationship with Monica. She wouldn't have come out with some of those comments to a reporter unless she could trust him. Some readers say it was one of the best stories you've ever written. I bet you worked really hard to get that exclusive.'

Miles noticed that his attempt to massage Goodson's ego had worked. His chest swelled and he had problems disguising his pride. But his response didn't change: 'no comment.'

'You certainly rattled a few cages here at police HQ with that story. Let's face it – you don't care if you upset anyone's feelings as long as you get a good story, do you?'

Goodson peered at the ceiling, a look of boredom etched on his face.

'Nae comment,' he said in a Scottish accent, wondering how many different ways he could deliver those two words.

'So, just to confirm,' Miles went on, 'you claim you don't know Monica Evans even though you must have spoken to her to get the article about how the police shot Ken Thompson. Allegedly without justification. Unless you stole the story from another source.'

'Of course I didn't steal it. It was all my own work. How am I supposed to remember every person I interview? Can you tell me the names of every single person you've arrested?'

The solicitor put his hand on his client's arm – but Goodson shrugged it off.

'Moving on,' Miles said, knowing Goodson was flustered. 'What can you tell me about the dark clothing we found in the basement of your house?'

'No comment.'

'Will we find Daisy's, Alessandra's or Monica's DNA on those clothes?'

'No comment.' This time Goodson spoke in an Irish accent.

Miles brought up another photograph. 'Three jars with fingers in them. What can you tell me about those jars and their contents?'

'No comment.' This time there was a Cockney twang.

A picture of number plates. 'Ever seen these before? What would you say if I told you they're the same as the plates on a BMW car that's registered to a garage on Lenton Lane?'

Goodson let out a huge sigh. 'No comment.'

'Why did you leave your phone at home when you went out to cover those meetings on the nights the three women were murdered – didn't you think your office might want to get hold of you? What about your mother, all alone at home?'

Goodson jumped to his feet. 'You haven't got anything on me. You've planted all this evidence. Trying to fit me up. I've done nothing wrong. You'll never make this stick.'

'Calm down, Tony. That's enough,' his solicitor implored.

'Call yourself a lawyer? Do something – get me out of here!'

61

Calls were coming through to Miles in rapid succession.

First the pathologist told him that Goodson's mother had died of natural causes. Time of death was about twenty-four hours before Goodson's arrest. Miles had been wondering whether he'd have to bring another murder charge against Goodson. But the only thing he'd done was to neglect his mother.

Then the Crown Prosecution Service gave Miles the go-ahead to charge Goodson with all three murders. He punched the air in elation. Several of his team did likewise when he passed on the news.

The head of the digital forensics team was next. Goodson's laptop had been examined and his internet history contained searches including 'how easy is it to cut off your finger with a knife', 'steps to take if you have severed your finger' and common ways of strangulation.

Miles had difficulty deciding who was the worst of the criminals he'd met recently: Tony Goodson or Billy Phillips.

'Boss, you look a bit peaky.' Mark Roberts showed genuine concern for Miles who felt weighed down by his workload.

'I know what you need: a good laugh. Some of us are going to a comedy gig tonight. I put Paul Allen's name forward for a spot. He confessed to me once that being alone on stage, having to tell jokes and amuse people, was his ultimate nightmare. Let's see how the joker reacts to this. He'll either be wittier than he is during our investigations or he'll fall flat on his arse. If he does make an idiot of himself it'll be payback for all the times when he's had a laugh at our expense.

'There are a couple of other comedians on as well. They're supposed to be funny. So we should have a good night out one way or another.'

The comedy night in a city-centre pub was in full swing as Miles and his colleagues arrived after stopping off for a couple of pints on the way.

Smells of beer that hadn't been cared for properly, stale sweat and cheap aftershave were rife and several of the young men in the audience looked as though they might kick off if they weren't entertained to their satisfaction.

A comedian whose hair was receding at the front yet was long at the back and who sported a goatee beard – making him look a bit like Bill Bailey, Miles thought – stepped off the low stage to lukewarm applause.

Mark Roberts looked on with excitement and a touch of fear. He wanted Paul Allen to fail on his stand-up debut but Roberts put himself in Allen's shoes and knew how devastated he'd be if he made a fool of himself.

The compere, wearing a dazzling striped jacket over a black T-shirt and dark jeans, was eager to get the crowd pumped up for the next act.

'We like to bring you new talent and tonight is no exception. We're very lucky to have our next comedian because he's normally on the streets of Nottingham at night catching criminals. Be prepared for an arresting experience and cop a load of this: put your hands together for the original bad cop, Paul Constable!'

A few people in the crowd applauded, others booed and a couple who'd already had plenty to drink made pig noises.

Allen came out of a dressing room to the left of the stage and bounded towards the microphone in the centre. A single spotlight blinded him momentarily. He was feeling far from confident and hoped it didn't show.

He started by explaining he was almost late for the gig because police stopped him on the way. 'I was doing a hundred miles an hour at the time. The officers asked me why I was speeding. I told them that two years ago my wife

310

ran off with a traffic cop. When I saw the blue lights I thought he was trying to bring her back!'

The crowd guffawed. Allen grew in stature.

A few minutes later he had them in the palm of his hand. He told stories about things that had supposedly happened to him during his police career, such as when there were reports of a streaker in Nottingham's Old Market Square. 'Three elderly women saw him. Two had a stroke but the third couldn't quite reach!'

Without waiting for the laughter to die down completely, he continued: 'I arrested a man once and said to him "where were you between five and eleven?" "Primary school!"'

His fifteen-minute spot ended with a tale of a man who appeared in court and pleaded not guilty to the offence he was charged with.

'When he saw the jury of eight women and four men, he changed his plea. The judge asked him why. He said he didn't know there'd be women on the jury. "I'm married and I can't fool one woman, so how am I supposed to fool eight of them?" Thank you. Goodnight.'

The audience were on their feet and the compere brought him out again to take another bow as the applause, shouting and whistling went on for a full minute.

Roberts was the first to greet Allen as he joined his colleagues.

'Bloody hell, I never thought I'd say it – that was great. But what's with the Paul Constable alias?'

'I couldn't let them know my real name, could I?'

'You're a jammy bastard. If you fell in a pile of shit you'd come out smelling of roses. I was worried you'd throw in a few gags that might be considered . . . inappropriate.

'How did you do it?'

'You've got to be so careful these days. It's easy to upset someone so you can't do jokes about the Irish, people who are a certain weight, even the mother-in-law. What you have to do is adopt stories – tell them about you. Make a bit of a fool of yourself. The audience always like that,' said Allen who sounded like a comedy veteran.

'I knew I couldn't just get up there and come out with a few wisecracks. So I called in an old friend of mine. He speaks in public for a living. He also shows people how to inject humour into their talks. I told him what I was doing and he helped me to put this short session together. I'll ring him up tomorrow to tell him how well it went. Might get a full-length show together and take it to the Edinburgh Fringe next near.'

Roberts couldn't hide his admiration: 'Good for you. If ever you feel like quitting the force, I'm sure you could start a new career on the stage.'

62

After a couple of drinks Miles was thinking it was time he was going home. Tilly noticed the downcast look on his face.

'What's up, boss?'

'I don't think I can face the journey back to Derby tonight. It'll take forever on public transport and a taxi will cost the earth.'

'Well, you'd better stay at my place, then.'

Miles woke early the next morning, his head feeling slightly fuzzy and he regretted having that last drink.

By the time Tilly opened her eyes he'd showered, dressed and made coffee and toast which he set down on her bedside table.

She lived in a small but comfortable flat just outside Nottingham city centre. It was furnished in a minimalistic way, chosen deliberately by Tilly so that she didn't get too attached to a home in case she had a chance of changing jobs at short notice.

She also realised it was futile spending lots of money on her accommodation because she spent so little time there – one of the consequences of working long shifts on major crimes.

Miles was grateful that Tilly got up slightly later than he did. The flat had only one bathroom and they didn't have to fight to use it. That was one of the problems he'd had with his ex-wife Lorraine. They often wanted to use the bathroom at the same time and she would resort to banging on the door to express her annoyance at having to wait.

Tilly propped herself up against the headboard and gave Miles a heart-melting smile. I could get used to this, he thought.

Twenty minutes later Tilly was ready for work and Miles had washed up the pots. She drove them to police HQ. A look of tension appeared on Miles' face.

'Tilly, I think, to be on the safe side, we ought not to arrive together. Drop me off a short distance away and I'll walk the rest.'

'One thing wrong with that, Miles: you're still wearing the clothes you had on yesterday. I think you need to be prepared for a few comments about how it went last night.'

Miles was deep in thought, then exclaimed: 'Sod it! Drive us into the car park. I don't care who sees us together.'

Despite Tony Goodson being charged with three murders and Billy Phillips with murdering Felicity Strutt, Miles knew his team couldn't relax thinking their work was done. They still had to make a compelling case against both defendants so that a jury would be convinced beyond reasonable doubt that they were guilty.

Half of Miles' team concentrated on Billy Phillips. They discovered he had no friends and people living nearby reported his behaviour had become more erratic after his mother died. He had no other relatives apart from a couple of cousins who lived in the north east and had nothing to do with him.

The CSIs had prepared a full report on what they seized in Phillips' house: a saw, a meat cleaver and a stack of bin bags big enough to wrap body parts in.

Felicity's missing limbs were found in two chest freezers; a pathologist concluded she died from a wound to the back of the head and dismemberment followed.

Despite Tilly's concerns about the 77 bus being cleaned, Phillips' DNA was found on a seat on the night he dropped off the suitcase. And DNA lifted from Phillips' mother's car belonged to Felicity.

Mark Roberts spoke to Phillips' former employer who told him Billy was an odd character who paid particular attention when the butcher showed him how to cut up a carcass.

'He made customers uncomfortable. Me too sometimes. He wasn't good for business,' said the butcher. 'Eventually I had to get rid of him. I had absolutely no regrets about that.'

It seemed no one would say anything in support of Phillips. Even so, Miles had concerns that the outcome of the court case might not be exactly as he wanted.

The other half of the team were looking into Goodson's background as well as checking that all the evidence was in place. The DNA on all three women was on his clothing; the jars contained their fingers; his DNA was also on the false number plates which, James West discovered, Goodson had bought with his credit card from an internet site.

Mark Roberts was able to establish that, like Phillips, Goodson had no friends. His boss at the East Midlands Express spoke highly of him as an investigative reporter but few of his colleagues had any time for him. They all said they'd never gone to the pub with him after work.

This ought to be an open-and-shut case, Miles thought. Goodson had already tried to claim that the police planted evidence in his home. Would he resort to any other dubious tactics?

63

Anyone being introduced to Dr Selina Fairbrother might have thought her tiny build and thick-framed glasses indicated an introvert with a lack of confidence. But the practitioner psychologist had a steely, unshakeable manner which had been built by spending almost as much time in a courtroom as in a hospital or a clinic.

Miles had immediately turned to her to get an alternative assessment on Phillips. He respected her work; her reputation ensured that a court would take seriously any recommendations she made. She also spoke in language that Miles could understand; she never baffled him with medical jargon.

'Well, what do you reckon?' Miles knew his team had built a solid case but from experience he knew no one could be one hundred per cent certain which way a jury would decide.

She replied: 'You might be able to convince a judge that Phillips knew what he was doing when he kidnapped and killed Felicity. He suffered one of the worst emotions anyone can experience when she jilted him. I should know – I've had more than one relationship that's ended acrimoniously. I suppose I felt I could murder my ex-partners – but it was only a fleeting thought and I moved on.

'The problem is the fact that Phillips was diagnosed with this dissociative order. His defence will argue that one of his other personalities took over when he killed and cut up Felicity's body. They're going for guilty to manslaughter by reason of diminished responsibility.'

She continued: 'The prosecution will take my report into account and they may want to contend that Phillips' actions after he'd killed Felicity – his attempts to cover up what he'd done – should increase the seriousness of his sentence. But they may also decide not to contest the case. They may accept Phillips is guilty of manslaughter rather than murder.'

64

As a break from their busy workload Miles and Tilly watched as many Storm games as they could and were delighted when Derby kept winning. They cruised through games against teams in the lower half of the league table and always had something in reserve for when they faced opponents with similar play-off aspirations.

Cameron White was unstoppable most nights. He was averaging twenty-five points, seven rebounds and eight assists a game. The only way other teams could stop him was by double-teaming him and trying to prevent his driving to the basket. But when that happened his team mates stepped up, sinking shots both close to the basket and from three-point range.

The regular season ended with Storm in top spot and favourites to lift the Championship trophy in the play-offs at the O2 Arena in London. Winning that would give the team even greater credibility and boost their hopes of playing in Europe the following year.

In the play-off quarter-final the Storm beat Newcastle Eagles comfortably, winning the first two games of the best-of-three series. They maintained their impeccable form by overpowering Cheshire Phoenix in the semis to set up a clash with London Lions in the final.

The two clubs had met four times in the regular season, with each team winning their home games. Lions had taken the first encounter when Derby were still trying to gel as a team. The Londoners repeated their success later on when the Storm had two of their starting five on the bench injured.

Derby had beaten Lions twice at the Cloud Centre and had lost only once on their home court all season.

Miles and Tilly booked a few days' leave so they could stay in the capital and spend some quality time together.

They had good seats at the O2, "home to some of the world's most famous entertainment and sporting events", near the centre of the court and not too high, among a bank of Storm supporters.

The tension, excitement and anticipation were almost unbearable as the two teams warmed up. When the Storm's centre won the opening tip, White sprinted down the court, pulled up and nailed a three-pointer. Nothing but net. Only four seconds had gone off the clock.

Derby quickly established control of the game and were fifteen points ahead going into the last two minutes of the first half.

When the Storm missed a shot White, being more aggressive than he'd been at any time that season, grabbed the offensive rebound even though he was surrounded by taller Lions defenders. But he landed on an opponent's foot, lost his balance and fell, clutching his right ankle.

Medical staff rushed onto the court. A couple of minutes later White hobbled to the sidelines, his body supported so that his right foot didn't make contact with the floor.

The injury seemed to galvanize Lions who forced a couple of turnovers and hit three quick baskets to reduce the deficit to eight at half time.

White remained on the bench for the whole of the third quarter. London wiped out Derby's lead and were rampant, taking a twelve-point advantage into the final ten minutes.

Somehow the Storm began to produce their customary game and chipped away at London's lead. But the effort of getting within touching distance sapped their energy.

Derby's coach called a time-out with three minutes to go and the fans were on their feet when White limped back into the action. Would he be able to have any influence on the result?

On the Storm's next offence he was tightly marked. The move that the coach had drawn up appeared to be going nowhere until Derby's centre made a weak-side cut. White delivered an inch-perfect pass and a simple lay-up narrowed the gap to only two points.

As White made his way back down court to take up a defensive position the faces of the Derby fans were etched with concern because of his restricted mobility.

Lions decided White was the weak link and drove straight at him. But he'd stayed out of foul trouble in the first half and was able to pick up two quick personals to prevent London's point guard getting a free run to the basket.

When the Storm's centre fouled his opposite number rather than give up two easy points, the Lions' big man made only one free throw. London led by three.

The pain in White's ankle was relentless but he refused to show it and orchestrated another offence. His marker left him for a split second, White called for the ball, caught it behind the three-point line and in a flowing, uninterrupted move launched the ball towards the hoop.

The ball hit the rim, bounced up, hit the backboard and the rim again before dropping into the net!

With the scores tied and only eight seconds left, overtime beckoned. But inside, White was screaming with agony. He couldn't face another ten minutes of that.

London were desperate to get the ball up the court and were careless with their inbounds pass. White stole the ball but was quickly marked and had no chance of getting off a shot.

Realising time was on his side, he faked a pass one way before throwing the ball high above the rim for the Storm's centre to catch the ball and ram it home in one movement.

The buzzer sounded. Game over. Derby won by two points to secure their first Championship.

Storm fans among the capacity crowd of 15,300 were jumping up and down, hugging one another and rejoicing, making as much noise as they could with whatever was remaining of their voices.

It had been a stunning season for the Storm who won the league's team of the year, their playcaller won coach of the year and Cameron White was announced as player of the year.

Although White had given the police a few problems during the investigation into Daisy's murder, Miles wished him well for the future. White could have said he wasn't fit to carry on playing in the final. But he risked permanent damage to lead the Storm to victory. Miles hoped White's injury wouldn't prevent him landing a big contract the following season.

65

For more than thirty years Nottingham Crown Court on Canal Street had been hearing not just all Nottinghamshire's high-profile court cases but also some from neighbouring counties. The building on Canal Street, instantly recognisable with its exterior of buff stone and an atrium which looked like a plonked-on domestic glass porch, had replaced the old Shire Hall on one of the city's earliest streets, High Pavement. That had been turned into the National Justice Museum, formerly known as the Galleries of Justice.

The Lord Chancellor's department, when looking for a location for the Crown Court, County Court and Family Court, had opted for a site which used to be a factory and a baker's shop owned by Thomas Bush.

In 1870 The Times described Bush as a 'self-taught astronomer, mathematician and mechanic'. He was ahead of his time with his thirteen-inch equatorially mounted reflector, yet he'd been forgotten by many people in his birthplace – unlike some of the criminals who were sentenced at the Crown Court: Stewart Hutchinson, jailed for life for the murder of trainee hairdresser Colette Aram, the first case to be featured on the BBC television series *Crimewatch* which had begun in 1984; Mick Philpott for the manslaughter of six of his children in a house fire in Derby; and Christopher and Susan Edwards who murdered her parents, buried their bodies in the back garden of their house in Mansfield and stole her money which they spent on film memorabilia.

Whenever Miles went into court he thought about the cases that had had successful conclusions as well as the odd failure. He'd realised during one of his early appearances as a witness that the whole court process was a theatre, with everyone trying to give a BAFTA-winning performance. Whether justice was served was an entirely different matter.

What was that line from Shakespeare, he wondered?

All the world's a stage

And all the men and women merely players.

Miles greeted security staff who all recognised him. He placed his wallet, coins, keys, ID badge and everything else that he took out of his pockets into a plastic tray before walking through the archway detector. No sound emitted.

He saw there was a queue beginning to build of people waiting to be admitted – lawyers, reporters, witnesses, relatives of defendants and people who were merely interested in seeing the justice system operate at close hand.

He was walking up the stairs to the first floor – that was where all nine courts, barristers' rooms and secure places for defendants to have private discussions with their lawyers were located – when he heard a raised voice behind him.

'What do you mean, I can't take it in the court? It's a bottle of water!'

The long-haired, scruffily dressed man exhaled loudly, his confrontational stance similar to what Miles had seen countless times in a bar on a Saturday evening.

The security man spoke in a calm tone, eager to defuse any potential problem.

'Sir, I didn't say you couldn't take it in with you. We just have a few regulations that we have to comply with. You can keep your water as long as you take a drink first.'

'It's water! I'm hardly likely to cause any damage with that, am I?'

'For all we know, sir, it may contain acid. Take a drink, then we'll know it's water and you can come in.'

The man muttered something which Miles couldn't hear, took a sip and saw the security man smile.

Court number one was packed for the appearance of Billy Phillips. His case had been sent there from the magistrates' court. National reporters spilled out of the press seats into those normally reserved for the public. Journalists had dubbed Phillips 'the Nottingham butcher' and were eager to see if he looked as they imagined.

When Phillips was led into the dock he looked bemused by the strange surroundings. Dressed in a sports jacket, trousers, white shirt and sober tie, he looked like someone from the 1950s rather than a dangerous killer.

Shortly after ten o'clock the court clerk invited everyone to stand, a door opened and the judge walked to his position. Miles noticed the judge was taller than average, his bulky frame making him look huge and intimidating on the elevated bench. But when the judge sat down Miles saw a kindly, compassionate face. Would he be lenient with Phillips? Or would he give him a sentence which would satisfy Felicity Strutt's family, friends and colleagues?

With the prosecution accepting Phillips' plea to guilty to manslaughter because of diminished responsibility, Miles expected the case wouldn't last long.

The judge outlined the facts of the case including how Phillips had stalked Felicity and held her captive before killing her.

'You were evidently not thinking about the consequences of your actions. I have carefully studied the expert psychiatric reports prepared for the court and it is agreed that you are suffering from a dissociative disorder which contributed towards your behaviour. Your response to treatment has so far been limited.

'It is clear that you transformed dramatically from a relatively docile person into a violent individual, resulting in your dismembering Ms Strutt's body in an endeavour to hide what you did which was totally unacceptable.

'The psychiatrists have concluded that your condition substantially impaired your ability to exercise self-control. Therefore a diminished responsibility defence is available to you.'

The judge quoted guidelines which he had to adhere to when passing sentence.

He continued: 'From the starting point I would have taken if this had been a plea for murder, I deduct twenty-five per cent to reflect your diminished responsibility. I deduct a further twenty per cent to credit your early plea through your defence team of guilty. I also deduct the time you have spent on remand.

'William Montgomery Phillips, I sentence you to life imprisonment with a minimum term of seventeen years. I also direct that instead of being detained in prison, you will be held in a high-security hospital.

'Whether you will be released after that time is under the control of the Parole Board whose primary consideration is the protection of the public. Your counsel will explain the implications of this to you. Please go with the officer.'

Journalists rushed for the exit, anxious to get a place just outside the main door of the building so they could get a reaction to the sentence from anyone connected to the case. Miles held back, thinking about what he might say.

'I suppose that was as long as we could expect.' Selina Fairbrother had a resigned air as she approached Miles.

He was struggling to take in what he'd just heard: 'I suppose you've got to have sympathy for Phillips because of his condition. But I can't stop thinking about how he tried to dispose of Felicity's body. The cuts were clean, the limbs were removed intentionally. He knew what he was doing. He got away with murder.'

Selina asserted: 'A minimum of seventeen years – but there's no guarantee he'll get out then. Going to a secure hospital can actually be worse than a prison sentence. One of my clients – he's been in such a hospital for more than forty years. It's still evident he's going nowhere.'

66

Two weeks later Miles headed back to the Crown Court for the start of Tony Goodson's trial. About twenty people lined the streets trying to get a glimpse of the alleged serial killer – but all they saw was the van which transported him from custody into a gated area where the public weren't allowed.

Miles had lost count of the number of times he'd gone through the evidence trying to find a flaw in it, something that the defence could exploit. There was nothing.

The only disclosure from Goodson's legal team was that the police had planted all the evidence against the journalist who maintained his innocence throughout. Miles was baffled by Goodson's denials. Was this yet another example of his seeking attention?

Miles returned to the courtroom where Billy Phillips had been sentenced for manslaughter. He was more determined than ever to ensure Goodson wouldn't be able to wriggle out of a life sentence. He owed it to Daisy Higgins and her family to get Goodson convicted.

Waiting outside the courtroom to be called to give evidence, Miles came to a decision: if Goodson didn't go down for murder, Miles would quit. He'd had enough of a justice system which could be manipulated so that defendants didn't get a sentence their crimes merited. He would walk away if a serial killer like Goodson could hoodwink a jury into believing he was innocent.

When he was called in, Miles strode to the witness box, picked up the Bible and in a clear, loud voice recited the oath without looking at the words on the card in front of him.

He went through the evidence of all three murders in punctilious detail, explaining where each woman's body was found, the fact that their fingers had been removed and how Goodson had been placed at each of the murder scenes. After that the judge ruled the proceedings were over for the day and adjourned until the following morning.

Miles was only slightly fatigued by his time in the witness box. He knew he'd still have to face what could turn into an ordeal: cross-examination by the defence.

The next day Miles got up even earlier than usual and got to the court with half an hour to spare. He couldn't wait to get into verbal sparring with Goodson's barrister and prove how flimsy the defence was.

'May I remind you, detective inspector, that you are still under oath.' Miles had already decided he wasn't keen on the man he was facing, a natty dresser who wouldn't look out of place on the pages of a glossy magazine advertising the latest menswear or expensive aftershave.

Don't let him get to you, Miles told himself. 'Thank you. Yes, I know I'm still on oath. And I promise to tell the truth, the whole truth and nothing but the truth.'

The barrister looked down at his papers and appeared concerned before asking his first question: 'Inspector, what's your opinion of journalists?'

Of all the questions he was expecting, Miles hadn't anticipated that one.

'Like any group of people in any profession, some are good and some are bad. I've dealt with a number of reporters since I joined the police and I've met all sorts.

'A lot them are hard-working, driven but conscientious men and women who want to tell their readers or viewers or listeners what's going on in their locality. Often the management gets in their way and doesn't give them the time or resources to carry out their job efficiently. Journalism has changed – but not necessarily for the better. I suppose that's regarded as progress.'

'And what about journalists who are accomplished at getting exclusive stories?'

Miles saw where the line of questioning was going.

'I have great respect for and congratulate any reporter who can come up with an exclusive. Especially if they're holding someone in authority to account. As long as the story's true and was obtained legally, I've got no problem with that.'

The barrister again delved into his papers to produce a copy of a cutting from the East Midlands Express. He gave it to an usher who handed it to Miles.

'Do you recognise this story, inspector?'

Miles looked at a photograph of himself holding a basketball aloft and preparing to hurl it. The picture was staged after Miles had thrown a ball at crime boss Ken Thompson who was holding a knife to Monica Evans' neck. The police press office had urged Miles to comply with a request from the Express to recreate the moment when he'd distracted Thompson, allowing armed police to open fire and kill him.

'Yes, I do.'

'Your actions on that day didn't go down well, did they?'

Miles was careful not to give anything away.

'Do you mean with the public? I had some positive comments from people who said I should be proud of what

335

I'd done. Not that I was. It's always tragic when someone loses their life.'

'I was thinking more about your bosses. The Chief Constable, for instance. He wasn't very happy, was he?'

Miles thought back to the dressing-down he'd had in the Chief's office. But how did Goodson's barrister know about that? Was he just trying to trip Miles up?

He turned to the jurors and replied: 'The Independent Office for Police Conduct found that everyone in the case acted in the correct way. The inquest recorded a verdict that Mr Thompson was lawfully killed. I have no concerns about my actions on that day.'

'And did the Chief Constable agree?'

'He . . . felt it was unfortunate that Mr Thompson had to lose his life.'

'Going back to the article. Do you know who wrote it?'

Miles thought he remembered there was no name on the story. A glance at the cutting confirmed it.

'No. I have no idea.'

'Come now, inspector, you know as well as I do that the article was written by the defendant.'

'That's the first I've heard.'

'It's my contention that you knew Tony Goodson had written it. And because you were vilified by your bosses, you vowed to take revenge on the defendant.'

'There was no byline on the story. I had no idea of knowing who wrote it.'

'But you must have conversations with journalists nearly every day of the week. What was to stop you asking one of them to find out for you who wrote that story? And when you knew who it was, you were determined to make him pay for trashing your reputation.'

Miles again addressed the jury: 'Until a few moments ago I did not know which reporter had written the article. The only thing I blame myself for is agreeing to pose for that photograph.'

'So you say. Haven't you distorted the truth, inspector? You were adamant that the defendant had to pay for writing that article. When those three poor women were murdered and you hadn't got a clue who'd done it, you decided that you would frame my client and plant evidence pointing to his guilt.'

'No, sir. That's not true.'

'Admit it, inspector: all your evidence is circumstantial. You arrested the wrong man.'

Miles wished he could pin the barrister against a wall and explain what an evil reprobate he had for a client. Unclenching his fists which he made sure were out of public view, he calmly said: 'We arrested the right man. All the evidence points to his guilt.'

67

The trial continued for four weeks. Goodson sat alert, occasionally passing notes to his defence team and doing his utmost to remain the centre of attention.

Whenever a witness said anything derogatory about Goodson he tutted and shook his head. Miles watched him most of the time; he hoped the jurors weren't swayed by Goodson's mannerisms and would reach the proper verdict after considering the evidence.

The prosecution concluded its case and Miles expected Goodson wouldn't appear in the witness box. The case against him was so strong that Goodson could only make things worse by subjecting himself to cross-examination.

To everyone's surprise the defence team called Goodson as their main witness. He preened and postured, making out he'd never committed a sin in his entire life. He was the victim; it was despicable of the police to link him with the deaths of the three women. He had no motive for killing them.

He knew nothing about the fingers found in the jars in his basement, the mobile phones or the number plates. They were presumably put there by the police after he'd been arrested. When the trial was over he'd be taking action against the police for unlawful arrest and malicious prosecution.

Any optimism Goodson might have had about being acquitted evaporated when the prosecution barrister made his closing speech. He labelled Goodson an evil fantasist who took pleasure in strangling women before chopping off their fingers. He didn't know whether that was to try to put police off the scent or if Goodson wanted the fingers as a trophy. Whatever his motivation, it exemplified that Goodson was a dangerous serial killer whose arrest meant no other women would suffer a similar fate to Daisy, Alessandra and Monica.

Panic-stricken, Goodson jumped to his feet. 'My lord,' he addressed the judge, 'may I ask for an adjournment?'

The judge told him his request ought to have been made through his barrister but anyway declared that business was over for the day.

As the trial had worn on, Miles was unable to shake off the feeling that somehow Goodson would be cleared of the murders. His head said the evidence against Goodson was overwhelming – but his heart was telling him something else.

When he arrived the next morning there was a frenzied atmosphere in the corridors and outside the courtroom. Miles saw a friendly usher who always had time for a chat.

'What's going on? Don't tell me Goodson has changed his plea?'

'No,' she replied. 'But he certainly knows how to attract attention – he's sacked his defence team!'

The revelation startled Miles although he had to admit it could be a clever ploy: would it sway jurors into thinking his barristers hadn't presented his case properly? Or would they see it as a device to thrust Goodson back into the spotlight:?

Miles tried to remember something he'd heard Alessandra say about a similar case. What was it? 'A man who represents himself at trial has a fool for a client.' But would Miles be the fool at the end of the trial?

At the start of the day's proceedings Goodson confirmed to the judge that he'd dispensed with his legal team and would make the closing speech to the jury himself.

For the next two hours Goodson regaled jurors with a deeply critical yet reasoned attack on the police's handling of the case. Again he insisted he'd done nothing wrong and accused Miles and his team of planting evidence to discredit him simply because he'd held them to account as a responsible journalist.

Miles watched transfixed as Goodson delivered a performance which would have deserved an award if it had been acted out on a stage. He wanted people to feel sorry for him. Had he succeeded or did the jury think the prosecution had proved beyond reasonable doubt that Tony Goodson was a serial killer?

The queasiness in Miles' stomach intensified when the judge sent the jurors out to consider their verdicts. Could they be relied on to weigh up the evidence and reach the proper verdict? Or would there be one member of the jury who was persuasive enough to fight for Goodson's freedom?

Miles told himself he'd watched the film *Twelve Angry Men* too many times. That wasn't the same as this case – in the film a teenager was falsely accused of murdering his father. Here a callous killer had viciously ended the lives of three women and destroyed their families. He pictured Daisy's mum and Joey; would he ever be able to look them in the face again?

He couldn't face lunch – he just wanted the trial to be over as soon as possible. Tilly who'd been sitting alongside him for most of the trial took his hand. But she was powerless to lift his mood or dispel his fear about the outcome.

Three hours later the jury returned with their verdict. Miles' heart beat faster and faster – he could have been sprinting the full length of a basketball court instead of sitting motionless and powerless waiting for the outcome.

Had the jury spent enough time considering the evidence? After all, they were deciding whether three women had been murdered by Goodson. Should they have been out longer? Or had they come to a decision quickly, made the most of their free lunch and then taken a bit more time in the jury room so as not to give the impression that they'd acted hastily?

Miles thought that time had stopped as the clerk of the court asked the foreman whether the jury found Goodson guilty or not guilty of murdering Daisy Higgins.

The jurors had appointed a woman to speak on their behalf. She stood upright, her blue, two-piece suit which looked classy without being ostentatious giving Miles the impression she had a business background. Her hair was piled up into a bun and she wore dark-framed glasses which added to her professionalism.

She took a deep breath and announced in a voice that the whole court could hear: 'Guilty!'

Alessandra de Villiers? 'Guilty!'

Monica Evans? 'Guilty!'

343

Miles was ecstatic. The fear and trepidation that he'd been suffering subsided as he realised he'd been able to get justice for Daisy's mum and Joey.

Goodson who'd maintained his composure throughout the trial erupted. 'This is a travesty. I've been framed!'

He cursed the judge, the jury, the prosecution and the police, describing in graphic detail what he would do to them if he could get his hands on them.

The judge ordered him to be taken down and adjourned for the day. He would sentence Goodson the following morning.

68

Miles felt like skipping as he walked the final few steps towards the Crown Court. He knew Goodson would be sentenced to life in prison; it was up to the judge to say how long Goodson would serve before being considered for parole – if he would ever be released.

The judge, in his sixties and one of the most experienced in the country, wasted no time in starting his sentencing remarks. Maybe he's got a game of golf lined up, Miles thought.

'During two months of last year you attacked, sexually assaulted and murdered three women. Not only did you brutally strangle them, you also removed their fingers.

'Precisely why you did so only you will ever know. Whether you planned these killings in the minutest detail or whether they were opportunist attacks – again, we shall never know.

'What we do know is that these were three of the most savage attacks I have ever come across in all my years in the legal profession.

'After each of these killings you carried on with your work as if nothing had happened.

'There was a mass of evidence which established you as the killer yet you have come to this court and painted a picture of yourself as a victim.

'Thankfully the jury were not deceived and delivered verdicts with which I am entirely satisfied.'

The judge barely stopped for breath.

'I have considered the victim impact statements from family members, particularly the mother of Daisy Higgins. Not unnaturally she is still in a state of shock and devastation as to the circumstances in which her daughter met her death. Ms Higgins' young son will grow up without his mother's love and guidance, thanks to your unspeakable evil.

'You have shown absolutely no remorse and it appears you are in complete denial of what you did, notwithstanding the overwhelming evidence against you. The enormity of your crimes is profoundly shocking.

'The only sentence that I can pass in this case is one of imprisonment for life. Furthermore, the tariff is a whole life order.'

Goodson grew taller and a smile appeared on his face as he was led away.

Miles was thinking about what Goodson's future in prison would be like when he was staggered by the judge's next remarks.

'I wish to pay tribute to the police's handling of this case. It cannot have been easy to secure evidence with which to convict the accused and the circumstances of these three women's deaths were most distressing.

'The investigating officers worked tirelessly and methodically to bring this case to court. Meriting particular mention is Detective Inspector Davies who has been a key figure in the investigation and preparation of this case, going well beyond what could be expected of any police officer, and his role deserves high commendation.'

With Billy Phillips and Tony Goodson behind bars, Miles tried to concentrate on all the other cases that were designated to his team. Yet he still kept thinking back to those two criminals and couldn't put them out of his mind.

He was delighted that Goodson was destined to die in prison but he felt sympathy for Phillips who might not have killed Felicity Strutt if he'd been given more support at an earlier stage.

Tilly persuaded Miles they needed a holiday. A week in a warm climate would do them both good and Miles agreed with her suggestion that Lanzarote would be an ideal venue for a break.

A day before they were due to fly, they heard the news they'd been waiting for since the Storm had won the play-offs at the O2: the draw for the group stages of the Eurocup. Derby were in group A along with some of the most prestigious names in basketball including Israeli club Hapoel Tel Aviv, Joventut Badalona of Spain and Greek giants Aris Thessaloniki.

'Hey, look who we've got as well – Paris Basketball,' Tilly enthused. 'Maybe we could get a few days off to coincide with the game in France. I've always wanted to go to Paris.'

'Haven't been there for years,' Miles replied. 'It's a great place for a honeymoon.'

Tilly froze. She didn't know whether to throw her arms around him or check if he was playing a joke on her.

'What did you say?'

He was just about to repeat himself when his phone rang. He looked at the display and apologised to Tilly.

'It's Tom. Need to take this.'

The colour drained from Miles' face as he listened to Detective Superintendent Brooksby. 'Thanks for letting me know,' was all Miles could reply before ending the call.

'You look terrible,' Tilly remarked. 'What's up?'

'Tony Goodson. He's topped himself in prison.'

'How?'

'Convinced prison staff he was turning into a model prisoner so they didn't keep him on suicide watch. He was working in the laundry, managed to hide a few strips of cloth in his pockets and when he'd got enough he tied them together and hanged himself.'

'But why?'

'It's the ultimate act of control. He dictated when others would die, then decided when he himself would die. I know we got a conviction but I can't help feeling cheated. He should have spent the rest of his life in prison, not been there for only a few months.'

Before he could say anything else his phone rang again. Without looking at the caller's name he barked: 'Yes?'

'Miles, it's Stuart Bainbridge. Thought any more about that job offer?'

ACKNOWLEDGEMENTS

When I began to write *Storm Bodies* I was able to call on many years' experience working in the media, particularly the countless hours I spent in courtrooms reporting on all sorts of court cases. But the further I got into the book the more I realised I couldn't write it without help from a number of people.

First of all I'm indebted to Marcus Oldroyd. He's been advising me since I sat down to pen my first novel *Storm Deaths*. In the beginning he advised me on police procedure so that DI Miles Davies has credibility. He's continued to put me on the right track and has answered some basic questions. When a suspect is arrested, are handcuffs applied in front or behind? Marcus gave me the answer and you'll see the result in *Storm Bodies*.

Marcus has now left Nottinghamshire Police after 25 years and is running his own business, The Bureau Consultancy.

I'm also really grateful to Superintendent Suk Verma of Nottinghamshire Police, former superintendent Justine Wilson and Rod Repton for their advice on police matters.

As I began to delve into the world of psychopaths and the law regarding diminished responsibility I received tremendous support from Simon King, head of crime at solicitors Elliot Mather; Dr Kerry Beckley of Beckley Psychology Services; Laura Pinkney from Nottingham Law School; Serena Simmons from the School of Psychology at Nottingham Trent University; and Amanda Ball, principal lecturer in media law and public affairs at the Centre for Broadcasting and Journalism at NTU.

A big thank-you to Jo Healey, author of *Trauma Reporting: A Journalist's Guide to Covering Sensitive Stories* who gave me so much insight into how reporters should deal sensitively with victims of crime.

I owe a debt of gratitude to Carol Magor, Marie Acres and Louise Bostock for making sure my manuscript reads well, is logical and there are no spelling or grammatical errors. If you find any, they're my fault.

Thanks also to Dr Nigel D Chapman; retired Unitarian minister Chris Goacher; Mick Newbold and Clive Tunnicliffe for advice on motoring matters; Colston Crawford; and Jim and Jo Harris from the Masons Arms, Mickleover.

I couldn't do anything without the unswerving help and encouragement from my wife Sue, our son Sean who again came up with the fabulous cover, his wife Jo and their children Toby and Holly.

If you enjoyed *Storm Bodies,* please leave a review on the site where you bought the book or on Amazon. And please feel free to get in touch. I'd love to hear from you. Contact me via my website, www.steveorme.co.uk or search for Steve Orme Writer on Facebook, Twitter or Instagram.

Printed in Great Britain
by Amazon